*The*

# Shaver Mystery Magazine
# Vol 2 No 1 1948

## Richard S. Shaver
## Alfred Steber (Editor)

SAUCERIAN PUBLISHER
Original Sources in Ufology

**ISBN: 978-1-955087-52-0**

9 781955 087520

**2023, Saucerian Publisher**

# PROLOGUE

Returning to the classics in any genre is generally a good idea. This also goes for UFO literature. Rereading a book or reviewing old documents after ten or twenty years is a rewarding experience. You will discover new data and ideas you didn't notice before. The reason, of course, is that you are, in many ways, not the same person reading the book the second or third time. Hopefully, you have advanced in knowledge, experience, and intellectual and spiritual discernment. A good starting point is to reread the UFO classics to understand the more profound mystery of what happened during that era.

This title is scarce and hard to find these days. The Shaver Mystery Magazine originally was published by the Shaver Mystery Club. This newsletter published the first printed stories on UFOs and was a major forum for debates about the occult, Forteans, and Lemurians. As Ray Palmer promoted it: "dedicated to the further study of the hidden truths as presented in the fact-fiction stories by Richard S. Shaver..."

In essence, the Shaver Mystery is a collection of stories in which Shaver claimed to have discovered proof of an evil humanity in underground caverns. Shaver portrayed an alien race that resided in Earth's caverns before escaping, leaving behind two distinct populations of offspring: the "Teros," a benevolent group of humanoids, and the "Deros," or "detrimental robots," a vile race who tormented and devoured humans. The Deros were especially brutal to women. The tales encouraged the establishment of Shaver Mystery Clubs.

The present edition is an authentic reproduction of the original Shaver Mystery Magazine printed text in shades of gray. **IMPORTANT,even though we have attempted to maintain the integrity of the original work, the present facsimile reproduction may have missing letters and blurred pages, poor pictures due to the age of the original scanned copy.** This magazine has been formatted from its original version for publication. Great, but unpretentious, this issue is an extraordinarily rare symbol of what was going on in those early years of the modern UFO phenomena.

Editor
Saucerian Publisher, 2023

# *The*
# SHAVER MYSTERY
## MAGAZINE

Being dedicated to the further study of the hidden truths as presented in the fact-fiction stories by Richard S. Shaver, made famous in the past three years in AMAZING STORIES magazine.

## Subscription Price 50c per Issue

OBTAINED ONLY

THROUGH MEMBERSHIP

## THE SHAVER MYSTERY CLUB

# CONTENTS

Vol II.                    1948                    No. 1

*Frontispiece by* James B. Settles

## THE SHAVER MYSTERY MAGAZINE

is Published by
THE SHAVER MYSTERY CLUB
2414 Lawrence Ave.
Chicago, Ill.

RICHARD S. SHAVER, *Editor*          CHESTER S. GEIER, *President*

# ❧ EDITORIAL ❧

O UR efforts must be directed toward exposing a *threat to our survival!"*
That's a quote from the first editorial for the first issue of Shaver Mystery Magazine.

The forces behind that threat have managed to get further mention of any sort of the Shaver Mystery forbidden in Amazing Stories.

That leaves this little publication as the only weapon against that threat. A harmless little weapon, in truth. And apt to be snuffed out at any time. But as long as we can try, we shall.

If we get sufficient support from those who are interested in the subject of *survival,* we will be able to give you a much better value at a much lower cost. If not, we will fold our tents and leave the secret of the caverns to those who insist upon their secrecy.

*Don't believe that there is any secret!* That is what an enemy wants you to do. Don't believe in flying saucers, the flying saucers don't want to be seen. They are only spots in peoples eyes. Learned professors assert the truth of spots before the eyes as all of the flying disk rumour.

Well, there are twenty tons of the wreckage from one of those "spots" on an island off Oregon, and I listened to voice records from four eye witnesses, saw samples of the material from the wrecked disc-ship. Saw photos of big and little flying discs—heard and examined indisputable proof of the reality of those ships. They are visitors from outer space!

Who wants them kept a secret? Why do they want them kept a secret? The same forces who want the Elder caverns kept a secret—and those forces do not have the good of the common man, or any man of our civilization—at heart. Do those who help them keep this vast threat a secret understand that? They do not!

The greatest news story of our time kept a secret from the people! Why?

That "why" is the threat that every mind that contacts this "mystery" must sense immediately.

That threat we have set ourselves to fight. We can't do it without help. This magazine seems high priced for what you get. It isn't, but unless we get more readers, it will have to remain high priced. The cost is directly proportioned to the number of copies printed. The cost of type-setting, the whole process of getting ready to print, is just as great for one copy as for ten thousand. But the ten thousand bring in ten thousand times as much to pay for it with.

If you believe in the Shaver Mystery and the need for this effort, you will find a way to get us more support.

Otherwise we will just have to let them keep their caverns, their visitors from space, their ancient secrets—all the titanic value that the race of man is being mulcted out of by . . . who, what, where . . . we only know they do not have our interests at heart. To them we are cattle, or if not cattle, then enemies who must be made into harmless cattle.

When the Shaver Mystery finally folds its feeble wings and tucks itself away forever, men will have decided that nothing of value is worth trying for. Men will have taken the greatest of all sucker-skinnings lying down. Men will face a future devoid of hope, full of mass illusions rigidly holding their eyes upon . . . modern truth . . . what the Philcon called "scientific skepticism". (These bright young men hold that because you cannot prove, convict and take to prison the cleverer crooks of earth, that none of them exist. It is like saying that those tax-evaders who have not been convicted are not in existence. Anyone knows better. They would hold that since no-one can produce an intact flying disc, none were seen. These young gentlemen do not believe, by their own utterance, that the "Forces of evil and good are dramatically arrayed against each other as contending armies". They seem to think that such a view of earth life is a delusion of a deranged mind.)

APPARENTLY evil itself is a delusion, and does not exist as such, because you can't turn it into a brick and put it on exhibit. This type of mind is a mind which does not accept any need for struggle against evil.

To those of you who understand the Mystery, the cause of such action against a stf writer by stfans is very obvious. To them it is not obvious, for they do not believe they have ever had a thought which did not arise in their own brain. Personally I do not believe they have ever had a thought that *did*, but that is beside the point. Or is it?

These midge flies of science-fiction have laid their giant low, and will doubtless write "Seven-at-a-blow" across their belts, like the little tilars they are.

I hope some "teros" avenge the deed, but they have plenty to do without stooping to that. I ask them to stoop, because I think the cause is important. It is important that this effort to publicize the greatest and darkest mystery of our times goes on. It is more important than any little tailors' ideas of rigid control of what others should read and think. It is the most important symptom of awakening thought in our time. It is a dark time, however light you are told by the professors "modern" thought has become. It is a vicious age, with more terrible wars and mass murders and perversions of mass-thought than any other period in history. We are grown up in the conviction that we have emerged from the Dark Ages. We are "enlightened." Yet even Nero's massacres did not hold a candle to the Nazi's extermination camps. There is nothing we can do about it?

I say we can try, and it is vastly important that we do try no matter how futile and feeble our efforts appear.

For long cenuries the whole thought of classic times was buried away and forgotten, yet look at the influence those few surviving MSS from the ancient classical civilizations have had upon modern thought.

I see such a regeneration of the Elder thought from our efforts, and I want to fight for it. It is worth fighting for. The Classic thought of Greece and Rome is as a flea beside South America by comparison with the Elder culture. That culture must be brought out into the light and made a part of our education, our history, our race thought. It must not be buried behind the monopolist's selfish barriers. Some how we must save at least the fact of its existence from modern darkness.

We think a large and influential portion of our people are bamboozled into placid acceptance of a destroying evil. We want to free those people by giving them the truth. Or is it the truth. Or is it too late?

We think that to you our efforts are just as important as the efforts of the U N to preserve peace. We feel just about as futile as they must feel, from what I hear of their success.

But like them, we'll keep trying.—Richard S. Shaver

# ON IMMENSITY
## By RICHARD S. SHAVER

ONE thing you fellows who write to me never seem to get is the size of the ancient cavern world, what it means to us.

If you can leave your flat land thinking, and think of many surfaces one over the other, extending on and on, under the water as well as under the land . . . you begin to understand. But you can't really comprehend immensity, can't comprehend a pioneer job that has been going on for hundreds and hundreds of years and is still only begun.

There are a dozen nations from several different planets sending ships and

*Concluded on page 16*

# MANDARK

## By RICHARD S. SHAVER

*Continuing the Tremendous 200,000 word Novel*
*- - the true story of the Life of Christ*

### CHAPTER IV

NOW I, Richard Shaver, have to show you how the record of the migration shifted its doings from the vast work of the migration to the work of these two men, two elder scientists of a larger build than the Atlans one saw in the records of life on Mu. They had come to Mu for a purpose directly connected with the planets approach to the sun.

As I watched that tremendous work by the two mighty giants of an era lost in time's slow sweep, so far lost that there is no other written record of it, but the mystical phrases of the misleading religious works of our time—as I thought of the little sprightly imp-angel, my Nydia of the neighboring people of the God-caverns, beside me watching every ticklish adjustment of the antique mechanism which gave me the power to read again the ancient records of thought of men so mighty that a "God" is not an adequate description, I was conscious thus of three separate planes of existence. These were the thought of myself, my inner ego, second, my thought of those things around me, such as the solicitous Nydia at the controls of the "dream mech" (as the secret people call the thought-record readers), and third, I was conscious of the thought of those two Titans who were constructing a vast number of very mysterious mechanisms for the recording of data having to do with the approach of the planet to the flaming new sun in the sky. This last was the more vivid of the three, as the two Titans constructed the time capsule containing the seed of their race—the Messiah, and their consciousness of the empty desolation so soon to overwhelm what was yet the teeming home of a numerous, fecund and happy people.

The strength of the electric flows within the mighty God mech made the life of those two more vivid than had ever been my own life. I understood without really knowing very much about it what it meant to understand the intricacies of the construction of a device—a time clock set to go off after the lapse of a period of years I had no mental apparatus to concept.

I understood the vast seriousness of these two overgrown "softies" who were worried about the fate of men unborn for ten thousand years yet. Their reasons for this solicitous care for a future that might never exist was a peculiar one—one I would like to mention as it serves to demonstrate the immense differences between their life and our own. The reason was that if they did not do their duty by those unborn men of the race, a mental conviction of having failed to fulfill their oaths to the Atlan federation of states would become in time a mental block which would be noticed by their colleagues and would interfere with the proper development of their future among the Atlans. It was a refinement of delicacy of "self-interest" as applied to their relations with their fellow men—so much so that they were in truth not doing the work *for the* unborn men, but *for themselves alone*—for the happy and full development of their *own future* which would spring from a *clean, easy-to-see, mental conviction inside their own mind* that they had scrupulously and invariably discharged all their obligations to their fellow men. This was necessary *because* they used mental thought augmentation apparatus, so frequently that any *other* interior thought of their efforts would *show* the slightest rift (to friends and associates).

I understood the vast seriousness of these two dread and powerful men, who were still "softies" to a modern's way of thinking. For they were worried about the fate of men unborn for ten thousand years as a mother worries about a babe of her own bearing. Their logic was a strange compound of self-interest with rationalizations of the self-interest into a general attitude of beneficence toward all other beneficent life. They were used to thinking of *other* men as able to read their inmost thoughts, and consequently their thought took on a very friendly awareness of the needs and

● Illustration by Richard S. Shaver depicting life in the caves as he knew it.

rights of their fellows as a protective mental armor—the logical thing to think and do in their state of general awareness of each the other's thought was beneficence—for an oppressive or cruel attitude toward others would have been instantly noticed and brought down upon them the opposition of the others. Further than that there is little I can tell you of their thought, for it is full of a symbol and meaning too greatly complex, too *big*—for us to comprehend. Their simplest thoughts were full of a product of a vast knowledge of nature that is not ours to understand.

THEIR construction of the time capsule was in truth a bit of psychological care for the armor of thought they carried against their fellow men. They had condemned Adam and Eve and their seed to a horrible life—but they had made restitution in the far future, was to be their protective thought about the needed experiment. Such reactions were habitual with them and the building of the time capsule was due to this reaction of care for their own beneficent attitude toward all men of their kind.

Using great lifter beams of reverse gravity flow they conveyed to the deep chamber about the time capsule the great weight of weapons of the abandoned cities and set them up in many ways—some with automatic electric eye robots to protect the sleep of the infant from chance interlopers. Some they laid ready to hand for the young Messiah's growth to learn the use thereof. When he should rise from his long sleep and again rule earth as it should be ruled, he would inherit their best work.

So it was that the Messiah was born into a long frozen sleep within an incubator built by a god. Born of a love such as no modern man can conceive, of a compassion beyond our understanding. These things are written in a record of the thought of a God which I read deep in the bowels of mother Earth, shown me by the blind cave dweller, Nydia.

While the Messiah sleeps his lengthy sleep, let me tell you something of the story that is more believable than the story as presented in the bible—they are the same story—but how different new data I have, makes the story of the Bible.

All this is no more unbelievable than the simple word "infinity." If you think of all the full meaning of the word "infinity" when you look up at the stars some night—all the infinity of opportunities that the life of the far spaces present to life to become as a God—to become something infinely more than the simple robots of work and sleep that we men are—if you think carefully of the word "infinity", you will not find it so hard to understand that what I tell you is even more true than the book called "The Word of God." For thte true words of the Gods have not died—but live on in their works deep in the earth. It is only that the men who have written and cared for the bible through the centuries did not understand the whole story and have left out the important things or misinterpreted those parts which give the true story of the dreadful, infinite might of the Gods that has lost the "word" to us.

From this record I was learning some mighty big things. I knew already that DE force causes the evil we know as war. I knew tthat the radioactive particles like radium come from the sun and are the cause of age.

I remembered the following phrase from the bible:

*"And God saw that the wickedness of men was great in the earth, and that the imagination of the thoughts of his heart was only evil continually. Gen. 6-5"*

I realized that such phrases got into the bible from some old original bible, a work left by really wise men. I knew intuitively that the original book had been destroyed by evil men who feared its detailed information on the symptoms, appearance and cause of evil. I realized that our bible was but a substitution by such evil men of some other, innocuous book, for the original wisdom.

The vast past of my race was overwhelming.

I KNEW that in the darkest parts of sunless space, many worlds swim which are never struck by the light of a sun. They are frozen worlds; if a man from earth came upon one of them he would think it a dead world.

These planets are densely peopled! Swarming within the dark worlds were the many and varied races of those peoples who are known to us, through legend, only as the Gods. I knew them as I read that record, as my people—my ancestors, friends and children.

Those cities lie deep within and beneath the surface of the frozen worlds. At a certain depth in any large body like a planet, the heat of the rock cannot escape, as rock under pressure is the perfect insulator. Moreover, this heat accumulates and at certain levels it becomes very comfortable. I had thought that if one went deeper, this heat of the friction of pressure causd the rock to become molten. But this God-brain I was thinking with seemed not to think so, but that a molten condition was due to other causes, and the fact that any heat could not escape. He seemed to know of worlds where the core was not molten, but was lived in all the way through a planet. He had visited many such worlds, and now was getting ready to leave this planet he called "Mu."

The vast supplies of heat from the molten "pockets" of the depths of Mu gave them an inexhaustible supply of power to run the infinitely numerous mechanisms which make their cities the true and only paradise. Vast generators of beneficial rays and energy-flows, which cause life to grow amazingly in beauty and strength, hum constantly, and these rays and vibrants flood about the caverns. In the lights which only those Gods can light, both edible plants and many races of intelligent creatures grow in great profusion. Whether man is a lesser or a greater animal in these fecund greenhouse caverns, we do not know. I couldn't understand the myriad images and symbols revolving in that mighty brain, except in a vague and generalized fashion. But I did gather that man and many other animals found now on earth originated in these cavern city laboratories when Earth was known as "MU." And I learned that by deeper and vaster sources than the science from which Darwin studied to evolve his theory of evolution. These sources will be explained in these pages to your satisfaction, or to your discomfiture.

Men are one form of the many forms that belong to the children of the Gods. But we have lost our contact with the Gods.

Their cities form a vast, many-tiered net through all the warm under-rock of myriads of planets—dark frozen worlds out in space. Their peoples, wiser than our mind can vision, fill these cities with a pleasure we can only faintly grasp with our puny, deteriorated minds. They live in a constant, infinitely ecstatic Nirvana which they build ever brighter and better for all of them.

One of these planet-cities was the planet now called "Earth." Then it was called "Mu," or "Momoo" or "ERTA" or Terra." All of these names were in that recorded brain and I could not remember the exact reason for the existence of several names for Earth. Perhaps the several languages and astronomies of space had given it several names.

This planet unfortunately came within the attraction of a vast body in space, and that body was aflame with disintegrance. Now disintegrance is the enemy of life, and intelligent men everywhere, the true sons of Gods, want none of it within light years of them. For radioactives, such as radium are thrown off by all suns in fine division, and such radioactives gather in the body of all living things that grow within their light. And those radioactive particles never go out, like radium. They are the true cause of age in all living things, everywhere. Do you understand now why you never met a God—an immortal, face to face? Because there are no immortals near any sun. Neither are there healthy men in radium mines, though some men are foolish enough, or heroic enough, to work there. They do not stay healthy long. Our life under a sun is analogous to living within the deadly confines of a rich radium mine. That is how it is to a God's way of thinking. The Gods do not escape age entirely because all space is filled with the emanations from myriads of stars, but they do live for endless centuries, and grow as huge as redwood trees.

When one has seen their dwellings, their immense chairs and their space ships, one knows that there is no more valuable thing in existence than a thought-record of a God's thought. I am trying to give you what I learned from reading these records of thought mightier than a man can conceive existing.

AS I got it from their unconscious visualization on the ancient records, the surface of Mu was frozen solid with liquid air mixed with frozen water and other accumulated material of an age of drifting through cold space.

Their "city" was really a network of tremendous caverns reaching everywhere under the whole surface of the planet. but at a great depth. The whole thing was under one nominal ruler, but there were many subdivisions, and very little real strife among them. To my way of thinking, their whole life was one of play mixed with a fanatical concentration upon certain angles of science—for these pursuits were so intensely inviting to the sensual side of the nature of man as to be irresistible to their pleasure-loving souls. These pursuits were really the "science of pleasure," having to do with the manufacture of subtle variations of the synthetic animal electric which was the base of their ray science. They were not men as we know them, for they had little concept of the struggle which necessity imparts to our life—they had no material needs. Their life was devoted to learning more about pleasing each other, which rather incidentally included making each other healthier and more alive. For the pleasure vibrants they constantly indulged in and manufactured in a billion complicated variations and combinations were basically beneficial vibrants. To tell you of people who do not think in any way as we do—do not think of domination, of power, of study to achieve economic security—of work or of the need of escaping hard work—to tell you of a people who habitually think in channels entirely unrelated to any concepts that occupy *"your"* minds is very difficult. Almost the only common ground between the Elder race that sired us and ourselves is our own rather feeble pursuit of pleasure. We almos look *down* upon our entertainers and our female sex contortionists who are occasionally allowed to arouse our so-called "baser" passions—they did not look down upon such people in any way for *they* were the *leaders*—the true society, and a person's value to the state was almost wholly reckoned on his value to the senses. Beauty was in truth always, with them, the equivalent of an economic asset—and it was a virtue to display such possessions to the utmost.

Their young people continued in this playboy frame of mind to what would have been to us quite an advanced age—but they did not reckon age or time—they thought but little of it. Their equivalent to our age or time concept was a calculation of growth—and this calculation contained a variant factor—the size of a person, as well as his rate of growth, depended upon the age and size of his parents—and this was, in turn, dependent upon the age and size of their immortal parents.

Their young people continued in this pleasure-pursuit life until their minds became interested in something further in life than the gratification of youthful, ever-growing senses—then they became elders when they mastered one of the many sciences. This usually took place shortly before they reached a size where they were no longer welcome upon a planet grown too small for them—they then were graduated to an elder planet the next step up in their ever-growing immortal life.

SO you see, Ramon Seti was an Elder selected for the job of running a kind of nursery planet for the elder planets where young people played and studied a little—until their minds had outgrown the play desire and their romanitc inclinations had at last fastened upon a single individual as the fulfillment of their dreams. Then they settled down to work and were eventually selected by the studious elders to become a part of some Titanic immortals effort to plumb the depths and the heights of knowledge. This hunger for knowledge gradually usurped the youthful sexual urge in the Atlans—but never entirely, for they did not age, but only steadily grew greater in every way—mentally, physically, sensorily—and other ways you have no concepts with which to associate.

They lived in the warm depths of the rocks of many, many of the driftitng dark balls that are the planets that our astronomers *never see* as they are *lit* by *no sun.*

But, had Ramon Seti had the courage to know the truth and face it, he would have said: "The Earth will pass so close to the sun that almost all life remaining upon it, or within the caverns, will die miserably of the great heart." For so it happened. The best illustration I can give you of how this time appeared is to quote from Dante—which I will do. I am going to place in this book an analysis of Dante's poetry, for what it really is—a vast mistake made by Dante. For Dante had divine revelation, straight from Godhead—right out of the ancient books, over the dream-maker mech ray, from a student of the cavern life of Dante's day—and Dante distorted the whole of the vast information entrusted to him—as so many other Christians have done. Distorted that mighty story (the same I am trying my best to give you) into a picture of mysticism—of immaterial souls in immaterial burning hells, etc., etc.—as the orthodox religion of his day would have it.

The true picture was quite otherwise—Dante got the details of the end of Hellas—of Hell—the name of a part of the ancient world—of the death of the Gods themselves—of the end of the race of gigantic men and immortals who fathered the few little waifs of the burning that fathered the degenerate human race—yes—he got the details right—but he muffed the real message in a vast and unforgivably confusing way by remaining the orthodox and blind visionary who could not throw aside his concepts of Heaven and

Hell and teach and write the truth which he was told over the telaug dream-mech rays from the underworld. And humanity through Dante's mistake lost its chance to take the long road back to the life of the immortals—and we—you and I and all of the twentieth century—suffer all the ills of our life mainly because such men as Dante have always muffed the reality of the underworld—and written and spoken of it as though it were an unreal place of mysty, mystic souls—instead of the vast world of Titanic immortal building which it was, is, and still remains.

Dante's descriptions of rains of fire, of terrible parades of naked people under rains of fire, of Demons tormenting poor souls, of vast palaces of stone about which blow fiery winds, and in which burning people lie and gasp for breath, but find naught but fire to breathe—the whole gloomy picture of the Frozen Hells, the burning Hells, etc., etc.—is a picture of the End of the World. Taken from ancient books written by survivors of that terrible time of earth's first approach to the sun—that time when part of the immortal race of Earh died miserably of the heat of the sun, even in the deep caverns in which they lived—the heat slew them—those who had not been able to get on the ships that took to space's refuge all who could be taken. That terrible time when all the wisdom and beauty of a vast immortal race died miserably as dogs under the terrible nearing sun—Earth's surface was scoured clean of its age-old buildings, and its age-old ice. The liquid air which had lain in great seas upon its ice turned to vapor, then to steam, and scalded all the earth clean of life—and that heated air descended into the caverns (where none but their air made of melted liquid air—had ever reached before). The heat melted the ancient locks and let in that fiery breath of the sun down and down into the life-caverns of the immortals where the last of that great race had descended to escape the heat in case the earth should miss the full fire of the sun and pass on by it.

THEY knew it would for they knew the surface of the sun was repellant and not so terribly attractive as we moderns think (disintegrance is electrically repellant of all matter—integrance alone attracts—only the solid center of the sun is gravitational) and some few survivors wrote books, and made drawings of that time, and these antique books, at last unearthed again and read and understood by some latterday underworld students and transmitted over antique rays-of-wonder into the brain of Dante. (just as many dreams are made today). I have letters from many, describing dreams which can only be pictures of the immortal life—of machines and details of the machines—of levitators, telaugs—teleportation machines, etc., etc., many such letters—and Dante's dream was not an isolated thing). But his ability to weld his vast mistake (as to what was meant by his dreams) upon the education of the world as "revelations of God," (which it was). But how greatly different was the truth from what he mangled up into the Divine Comedy.

As a picture of that vast catastrophe to wisdom on earth—to life on earth—it has value—but not a great deal. For the truth of what happened and what it meant is so vastly different from what Dante imagined his dreams to mean, that the worth of what he has to say is obscured by his imaginary composition.

I have tried, in my poor way, to remedy this disaster to Earth's history (and know that I fail) for I, too, have my dero. (anciently called erinnyes, harpies, furies), and other distorted degenerate minds of the underworld hampering me for fear that I will disclose their presence and their deeds to a vengeful race of men. And so I would if I could—for they do us men of the surface continual and terrible injury, destroy our scientists with their rays, tamper the experiments of our physicists into meaninglessness with their mental distortion of his thought—and hold back and plague the human race to an extent believable only when you have been pursued by them. And many of our best are killed by them, and the rest are made into half-witted disguisers of the real catastrophe of their "absent-mindedness" lest they be dismissed for idiots from the faculty —for the absent-minded" professor is one of their products most manufactured—for they fear men's science—as we would kill the evil wights if we had their rays to reach them with is perhaps not a wrong conclusion of theirs, seeing the wrong they daily do us. The existence of a Messiah has a vast corroboration. We have given you a possible explanation. Another possibility, of course, is the re-visit of a well intentioned member of the God-race, either by accident or by intent to fulfill the ancient obligation which seems to have been the basis of the legend of the Messiah. It must be true that the Gods did re-visit earth, and there are many quotations to be had from the Bible and from other books that show that some space traveling race did visit earth several times long after the period of which we are speaking the time of Adam. From now on, we will try to give you earth history as we interpret it from the Bible and from other writings such as the Book of the Dead, Homer's Iliad, etc. The tale of the records of the ANCIENT CIVILIZATION FOUND IN THE CAVERNS, by me, is not expected to be accepted, though it happens to be true. So I have assembled, from the vast wealth of corroboration in old writings, those most pertinent, on which I could readily lay my hands. If you view our work with pure disinterest, without preconceived bias, I think you will agree we are a great deal nearer the mark than the religions of our past and our benighted present ever struck.

WE will skip the period of Noah and the flood for there are so many contradictory evidences and accounts of this particular period. Certainly there was a great flood, and it may have been true that Noah and family saved all the seed of life that was saved from the water, but one finds it difficult to believe in this story, even more so than the story of Adam.

For everything must have a beginning, but that man perished utterly except for Noah and his family and that this happened at the direct order of God is hard to figure, except as a later insertion to explain the utter lack of records for such a long period. Whether it happened as described in the bible or whether this destruction of the flood was not as wide-spread as generally thought is a point we will probably never determine.

\* \* \*

Quote from book "Forgotten Books of Eden"—translated from Mss. of first century—

"For in this western border, O Adam, there shall go forth from thee a seed, that shall replenish it, and that will defile themselves with their sins, and with their yielding to the behests of Satan, . . . p. 35, par 7—Chap LIII."

"And God commanded him to dwell there in a cavern in a rock, the Cave of Treasures below the garden. Book 1, Chap 1, par 9, page 5."

"Yea, the word that will again save thee when the five days and a half are fulfilled. Par 2, Chap. III."

"Then God in His Mercy explained to Adam that these were 5,000 and 500 years, and how One would then come and save him and his seed. Par 6, Chap III, page 6."

"Then came the Word of God to Adam, and said unto him—"Adam, as for the sun, if I were to take it and bring it to thee, days, hours, years and months would all come to naught, and the covenant I have made with thee would never be fulfilled."

"But thou shouldst be turned and left in a long plague, and no salvation would be left to thee forever. Page 18, par. 9. Chap. XXVI."

God said also to Adam:

"See this fire kindled by Satan around thy cave; see this wonder that surrounds thee; and know that it will encompass thee and thy seed—When ye hearken to his behest, that he will plague you with fire; and that ye shall go down into Hell after ye are dead." Page 30, Chap. XXVI, par. 9 and 10.

From "Secrets of Enoch" XXII.

2 Thus I saw the Lord's face, but the Lord's face is ineffable, marvelous and very awful, and very, very terrible.

3 And who am I to tell of the Lord's unspeakable being, and of his very wonderful face?

From "Secrets of Enoch" Chap. I, Par. 6.

And there appeared to me in my sleep two men, exceeding big, so that I never saw such on earth; their faces were shining like the sun, their eyes, too, were burning light, and from their lips was fire coming forth, with clothing and with singing of various kinds in appearance purple, their wings were brighter than gold, their hands whiter than snow.

From "Forgotten Books of Eden" Chap. LXXIII.

Then Satan, and ten from his hosts, transformed themselves into maidens, unlike any others in the whole world for grace—and they came up out of the river.

Adam and Eve looked at them also, and wondered at their beauty, and said, "Is there, then, under us, another world, with such beautiful creatures as these in it?"

\* \* \*

After the Gods finally abandoned man to his ignorant fate on earth, life probably went on over Earth's surface much as described in the bible account of the spread of life over earth after the flood.

THERE was this difference, though, and a mighty big difference. Men discovered the ancient home of the Gods deep within the earth, where their ancestors had lived so long ago before earth swam into the deadly light of the sun. The bible ignores this important occurrence, but numberless other accounts quite as creditable and of as ancient a source as the Bible do not ignore it. There are the numberless legends of the Gods which are obviously of periods following the time of Adam, of time reaching down almost to the period we call "Medieval." The Archetype of this legend is the "Pomegranite Legend" of Cere's daughter Proserpine, stolen by Pluto and taken to his UNDER-WORLD kingdom. This underworld kingdom, which still exists today in secrecy, is the part of history which we wish to correct. They existed, not mythically or mystically, but actually and in the flesh. They played an immense part in the events of history, but the fact has never received any attention from writers for several reasons. One reason was fear, for any one who spoke of the underworld familiarly was accused of witchcraft, ot being in league with the devil, etc. The Christian accounts of history include it only as the abode of Devils, and most of them seem to think of it as non-existent except in the mystical sense in which they think of Heaven—which, looked at with a Literal Eye, translated from their thought as "Heaven and Hell exist, but they don't exist."

Well, we know now that they both existed actually and literally, and not mystically at all. Heaven was the wonderful place in the sky where the Gods lived, and Hell was the place under the earth where the Gods had once lived, and which was now inhabited by an evil race, as well as by people who were not evil at all. Both did exist and both still exist. Both played their part in history, but this book is principally concerned with the role that Hell has played in history. Hell was the name given the underworld by the church. It has had many other names, for Hell is a vast network of caverns extending over all the earth at great depth, and I have seen some of these caverns. Many other men have seen them, some like Dante in a dream, others like Aladdin in the flesh. I saw them actually, and this book is the logical deductions of what history must have been, arising from my positive knowledge of those caverns awefilled, mysterious and TITANIC actuality.

To show that Noah, if he existed, if the flood was as described and Noah the chosen seed from which all men are descended—then this also bears out our contention that in those days when the sun was younger, men lived much longer, and that in these days, what are now called "the Latter Gods", rose to power over earth—I will quote from the Bible:

*Gen. Chap. 9, 28 verse.*

*"And Noah lived after the flood three hundred and fifty years."*

*V. 29—"And all the days of Noah were nine hundred and fifty years; and he died."*

Now, if men were still able to live around a thousand years, and the sun was not so deadly as now—which everything we have learned points out—it leaves an opening for this deduction. Somewhere on earth, men living that long would develop some kind of wisdom greater than the tending of sheep and the raising of cattle, which apparently was all Noah learned to do in nine hundred and fifty years of life. Well, every writing of that time bears out that fact. Men did learn tremendous wisdom, and some men were known as immortal and did live much longer than other men and have powers spoken of as MAGI· CAL.

The legends of the Gods of Greece, of Rome, of Persia, of the Norse Gods, of the Germanic Gods, of fairies, gnomes, trolls, sorcerers peris, etc., etc., all bear out this deduction. Men knew great science and had God-like powers long, long after Noah's time.

Now, who should such powerful creatures die out and disappear. And if they knew so much, why did they not leave earth and the creeping death from the sun's radium, polonium, uranium, etc., from the radioactive powder thrown by the sun? Or were those creatures men?

I CAN only tell you certain facts and my deductions from those facts. I can only quote the ancient writings and those only represent the tiny part of the existent writings which I have had time to examine. For the most part such valuable texts are hard to examine. You can see the Book of the Dead if you know someone.

And the long life, the endless ages of life in caverns under the frozen surface of earth as the planet drifted its slow way through sunless space, had made the God race peculiarly susceptible to this mental derangement (Note here the persistence of the ancient usage of DE). And a Devil God is a hard thing to fight, for he knows a great deal about fighting weapons and their use, even with addled wits.

BUT you can't read a book behind a glass cage. Do you know anyone who ever took the Book of the Dead in his own two hands? Do copies exist? They should be published. But there is plenty of corroboration for our views of these times, and widely read students will at once see the immense fitness of our contentions as to what lay behind the events of these times—compared to the usual interpretation which is either mystic, supernatural or pooh, pooh's the essential meaning of the whole mass of writings from the past.

The truth is, there is a certain amount of truth in each of these views, but not the whole truth. What we want to do is to give a clearer picture of the vast whole truth behind all the writings as well as show what these caverns under our feet and the miraculous capacities of the machines mean to men.

*Gen. Chap. Eleven—the last verse.*

*"And the whole earth was of one language and one speech."*

Bears out our contention that all language was at one time the mother tongue, which we call "Mantong." It follows that all earth's languages were descended from the single mother tongue.

The fact that the Alphabet key given in this book, can be used with equal facility in any language we take to confirm that this question is one of the original remnants of the first bible which still exists on the surface, and that the parts following this quote are insertions put in at the time the fake bible was foisted upon the people by the priests who feared the wisdom which still lived within the words of the words of the ancient Book of the Cross, the T book.

For it revealed the nature of a man, whether evil or good, giving infallible signs, and would have exposed the tricks whereby they fleeced people. Likewise it would have exposed the existence of the "magic" machinery in the depths of the earth by use of which they worked miracles and other deeds which built up their power over the wealth of the people.

If we quote some parts of the bible as significant and ignore other parts as of no significance—this is the reason.

To show that the sun was rapidly growing more and more detrimental to life, and that man aged more and more, we will quote from the eleventh chapter of Gen. the 32nd ver.

*"And the days of Terah were two hundred and five years, and Terah died in Haran."*

But between the time of Noah's death and the death of Terah are but two chapters of the bible, but a few hundred words. But from what we know of life, for men TO CHANGE SO MUCH THAT THEY LIVE BUT ONE FIFTH AS LONG must indicate an immense lapse of time. A time of many, many thousand years at the very least. But of all this time, nothing is found in the Bible. So we will turn elsewhere for this record.

**. . . Jove returning to his palace home; Where all the Gods uprising from their thrones, at sight of the great Father, waited not for his approach, but met him as he came.**

**And not upon his throne the Goddess took His seat, but Juno knew . . .**

                                                            **Bryant's trans. of Homer**

WITHIN the caverns, the race of the Latter Gods lived their lives, watching the surface life, with its shepherds, its wars and its pitiful weapons. They watched over it with the ancient telepathic augmentive vision apparatus, which, in the caves, takes up a great deal of wall space with its great ray television screens. Sometimes they took a hand, but oftener, as they watched it with the attitude with which we watch a newsreel, they refrained for sheer lack of interest. There was nothing more interesting to watch was not true. There were the great old record mechanisms, their "dream-mech" full of vastly more entertaining spectacles of the terrible and tremendous life of the Elder God race. They made but little attempt at rational communication with surface life, which knew of them and feared their power, and often seems to have despised them and understood their limitations.

Keeping on with Homer, who is perhaps as good an authority as any, we will quote—to show the power of those invisible beings whom they called "the Gods"—and whose invisibility we will explain as resulting from their practice of talking to the surface men over the penetrative ray equipment with which the ancient caverns were so numerously and so well equipped that some of it exists even today. Homer himself did not apparently think these Gods so immortal or superior:

*Followed Tydeus, who with cruel steel sought Venus, knowing her unept for war,*
*O'er taking her at last, with long pursuit . . . aimed at her his spear*
*And wounded in her hand the delicate one with its sharp point. It pierced the*
    *ambrosial robe, (?)*
*Where the palm joins the wrist, and broke the skin,*
*And drew immortal blood. (!)—the ichor . . .*

Note that Tydeus was just a plain mortal warrior, yet wounded the Goddess. And, bearing out our idea that they, the Gods, did not eat as we do, knowing that most food contains radio-actives causing age from the sun, Homer says:

*For they, Eat not the wheaten loaf, nor drink dark wine; And, therefore, they are bloodless, and* are called immortal.

Anent the last line, the underlining of "ARE CALLED" our own, it bears out a deduction of ours, written in other writings, that the immortals used some combinaion of perfusion or nutrient methods as used by our modern Alexis Carrel in his well-known immortal heart experiment, as well as in many other experiments of a similar nature.

It is obvious, if you grant any of our premises, that the original Gods knew the cause of age, and that their methods of fighting age would be learned by the Latter Gods, follows, when one knows the caverns have been inhabited by various secret groups since the earliest times down to the present day. That they used a synthetic blood to defeat age is not more improbable than many things we know to be facts. That they were not supernatural but could be wounded and killed, is obviously general knowledge in Homer's time. The Gods were just a superior, hidden race to Homer, and not too superior, at that, from his words.

Their methods of rule, which some of their defendants and would be imitators today follow as well, are described by many passages of the type I quote:

*"Minerva swift descended from above,"*
*(For both the princes claimed her equal care)*

Another place:

*"And hence to all our host it shall be known—"*
*"That kings are subject to the Gods alone."*

another, plainer—

*. . . Know, if the "Gods" the beauteous dame demand,*
*My bark shall waft her to her native land.*
*But then prepare, imperious prince, prepare,*
*Fierce as thou art, to yield the captive fair:*
*Thy lov'ed Briseis, with the radiant eyes . . .*

Now to go on with the nature of these latter Gods as revealed by Homer:

*Diomed  . . small regard had he for the great God,*
*The archer of the skies, Apollo,*
*When he made the fourth assault . . .*
*Apollo thus rebuked him.*
*"Diomed, Beware, desist, nor think to make thyself the equal of the Gods . . .*
*The deathless of Gods race is not as those who walk the earth."*

With words, you note, Apollo stayed the mortal's sword,—out of pity (?) one gathers, or mercy not to slay him. But was it that? Or simple subterfuge, getting himself out of a tight spot—and cursing at the folly of being caught above earth by these solid-muscled surface men.

That they were men, and only men, we gather time and again as in . . .

*. . . And Polypheme, and Theseus, and the son of Laertes, likest to the immortal Gods.*

If a mortal man could look like an immortal God, why then the Gods were but men, to my thinking.

SO we say that these Gods who were worshipped by the historic Greeks or their ancestors were men who lived in the caverns whose existence we but now fully learn of, and used the antique machinery left from a still earlier time when the Gods were really Gods in wisdom, and perhaps not men at all in shape. To my knowledge the original elder races were about an average of twenty feet, and were not all manlike but of mixed origins of different shapes. Their terrific fecundity and stimulating rays overcame the tendency of the hybrid to sterility, so that they were hybrid of races both manlike and unlike men.

They lived principally by foisting a God-pretense upon the people as the real thing

—and it *was* in effect for the antique weapons and mighty mechanism of the vast and ancient science gave them the powers that made them comparatively as Gods to the ignorant men of that time. This deceit has gone on right down to the present day. though it seems today their profits by which their luxurious, riotous, cruel and wasteful life is financed come from other schemes than the God's temple's contributions, though who can say what cult pays the hidden people or how much even today for projections from the miraculous rays and thrills in the spine from the stim organ.

But, today, such ray groups work another "wool" upon the credulous surface men. This "wool" consists of telling surface groups they are the powerful secret service, a special telepath apparatus equipped group, from the surface government—using the products of the super secret science of modern development to protect the liberties of which we are so proud, but would not be so proud if we knew what went on under the surface of our apparently secure modern ways of life.

For, under our feet, many surface men die on the rack, or over a slow fire, or in any one of a myriad modern refinements of the medieval torture we suppose long vanished from our daily life. Most of those who have had cursory contact with modern secret ray, or the underworld science are sure that it is "modern" science, but the truth is, it is a survival of the ancient priest, satanist and witch cults who have always been a much greater power in surface life than is understood by most writers. Michelet so understood, but did not realize the titanic value of the antique mech which was the root of that power. Chiefly this fact has been concealed by man's incredulity of the unbelievable circumstances surrounding the continued existence of the antique magic, the extremely ancient and tremendously wise science which built the imperishable mechanisms, the endless area of the underworld where Hell was once a living fact and still today has its modern counterpart. More than one little hell holds forth down there hidden by the black secrecy that has swathed this life since the last God left Earth forever.

But, in that day, life had some bright facets. and one of these was the goodness of certain groups of the Latter Gods—the hidden peoples.

"*There as they tell—the Gods securely bide*
*In regions where the rough winds never blow*
*Unvisited by rain or snow,*
*Veiled in a volant ether, ample, clear,*
*Wherein the happy Gods, from year to year,*
*Quaff pleasure. To those bowers Athene made repair."*

---

# ON IMMENSITY
Concluded *from page 5*

forces to trade and explore and loot— there are ports where a dozen space ships lie up and load the antique treasure and take off—and there are parties traveling on and on through level so and so, while under and over them, in tier on tier, are other levels untouched by man since the Elder time.

It is a world beyond comprehension, laid open to alien exploitation, before which our own government stands aghast with incredulous disbelief while all the treasures of the ages filter away beneath their impotent, "fundamentalist" hands. While a nation of readers ponder the "shaver Mystery" a nation of soldiers and merchants miss the whole import—the vast new golden frontier which they must win to live.

To live, that is, as free men, as well and healthy people—and not as slaves and worse than slaves.

The "underworld" is an old, old world, and it still commits our crimes— those unsolved and unheard of crimes which change a man of wealth in the night to some one else who takes over his fortune and his life.

But that is the least of the cost of our ignorance of the existence of the underworld.

That world is more important than our surface world, and unless we awaken and get in there, it may engulf us. It will do so when enough men are down there who decide they need to take us over.

# ATOMS AND THE BRAIN

## By ROGER P. GRAHAM

IN THE Science News Letter for June 7th is an article entitled Cosmic Rays Make Carbon. The gist of that article is that a large percentage of the carbon in your body is radio-active carbon made from nitrogen, and that the carbon compounds containing it will find themselves with a nitrogen atom in place of a carbon atom at almost any time, disrupting because the chemical properties of the nitrogen atom are different.

If the soul is a complex hydro-carbon molecule as ROG PHILLIPS advanced in his mutant stories it would not be so immortal if it contained some of these radio-active carbon atoms! Be that as it may, it is now a proven scientific FACT that the ONLY way you could prevent radio-active carbon from forming a crucial part of your chemical makeup is for the race to live far underground and eat plants whose carbon atoms are from sources that are millions of years old,—from carbon that has BEEN carbon for millions of years.

The article says, "What role this ray-created radioactive carbon plays in our lives nobody knows, for its existence has only just been discovered." Hmmm. I wonder what effect it would have on the mind for a carbon 14 atom to change to a nitrogen atom in the exact spot in the brain where the inhibition NOT to kill has been built up???? For that matter, what effect on the THINKING does the disintegration of dozens of those atoms in the brain and the consequent disruption of the neural molecules they are a part of have???? Hmmm????

There's a guy named Shaver,—a perfect screwball, so they say,—he said something about dero thought and sun poisons. What was it? I knew just a moment ago, but I felt a sharp pain in my head and then I forgot.

There was something else,—oh yes! I wrote an article myself a while back in which I advanced the idea that cosmic rays are produced by high velocity electrons from the sun striking the surface of metal meteors in space. That's only within a few millions of miles of HOT suns, though. Funny how things tie together. Even funnier how scientists are finding out things lately.

It was pretty cute the way Anderson, Libby, Weinhouse, Reid, and Kirshenbaum proved that SURFACE carbon has a lot of C-14 in it. They took methane produced in the Baltimore city sewage disposal plant and put it in a big tank. They took an equal amount of methane from crude oil that had been underground for millions of years. The gieger counter, (good old geig. Hope there isn't a strong geig storm over the fourth) told the story.

In the June 14th Science News Letter there was another interesting note. Heart of Atom Holds Three Science Mysteries.

The three mysteries are, (1) What holds the protons and neutrons together in the atomic nucleus? (2) Why are electrons ejected from the Nucleus which does not contain them? (3) Just what is a meson or mesotron?

GIANT HIGH VOLTAGE MACHINES ARE BEING BUILT TO SOLVE THESE ATOMIC SECRETS.

Just for the record, I'll give the answer to those mysteries here. The proton is a sphere of positive primal mass substance with a lot of small spheres of negative mass substance dotting its surface:—over a thousand of them. These negative particles are the ordinary electron. Calling the large positive mass a super-positron, then the proton is a super-positron with enough electrons or negatrons IN CONTACT with its surface to bring the resultant field down to a strength about equal to that of the single electron, but opposite in kind.

A neutron is the same thing but with enough electrons dotting its surface to make the field neutral.

When a neutron and a proton JOIN, one of the eighteen hundred or so electrons on the neutron surface ties to the proton surface also.

From a relatively great distance the field of the neutron is neutral, (strictly gravitic), and that of the proton is of a positive intensity equal to the negative intensity of the free electron. BUT, when you get down to distances from the surface of these two particles that are fractions of their diameter, the fields are patterned, with attracting, repelling, and neutral zones. These come into play when a neutron and proton are coming together or separating.

Any free electrons produced will leave either a doubly charged proton from a proton, or a proton from a neutron.

The simplest atom, Hydrogen, consists of a super-positron with over a thousand electrons in contact with its surface, and a single orbital electron.

There are simple positrons the same size as the electron. The pressure of the ether on the surface of a positron is less than it is on an electron. When the two come together this pressure difference on their opposite sides makes them assume a speed sufficient to equalize that ether pressure. This positron-electron pair with its high velocity produced by difference of ether pressure on the two is the mysterious meson. It is also this difference of ether pressure that forms the mechanism of energy production in atomic disintegration,—NOT conversion of mass.

That's just for the record. I don't expect you to believe me YET.

By the way, here's an angle about the caves that Dick seems to have missed in his writings. You can find it in Secret Doctrine by Madame Blavatski.

According to her the cavern people have time after time salvaged books from the surface and have them stored in huge libraries under the surface all over the world. And SOMETIMES, after they got what they wanted, the reigning kings would get a sudden yen to destroy all the books he could find so that the people wouldn't know so much,—the SURFACE people. Wonder where the kings got their yen?

Anyway, she says that every book that has ever been written, from the FIRST WRITTEN RECORDS LEFT TO MAN BY THE ANCIENT RACES OF TITANS AND ATLANTEANS (ATLANS???), is still in existence, and the cave people "plan to give them to the world at some future time when we are worthy of them". Meanwhile they keep them secret "for our safety."

Dick said something about their secrecy once. Funny I can't remember. A sharp pain blotted it out. Must be something I et, no doubt. Why don't you get Blavatski's Secret Doctrine and read it? It may not make a theosophist out of you, but it will show you that Shaver isn't he only one who says here are ancient caves and underground races and ancient knowledge kept secret from us, and even ancient machines.

You'd be surprised how many very important people come right out when I ask them and say that Shaver is telling the truth. They read him and keep their mouths shut. They don't write letters. They are afraid to get mixed up in it. But they *know*, and, strictly off the record, they sometimes get quite frank and communicative.

Do *I* believe Shaver? I don't even believe *I* exist. I don't HAVE to believe I exist, but I work on the assumption that I do. Also I don't believe I DON'T exist.

However, I am labelling Dick Shaver's writings with the same degree of probable truth as I label the newspaper and photographic accounts of the war we have just gone through. Do I believe we were in a WAR? No. Do I believe we WEREN'T in a war? No. I'm a funny guy. I just can't see the necessity of making anything an article of faith if it is obviously in accordance with all known facts, and I can't see the necessity of making a thing that ain't so an article of faith either.

> With this issue of the Shaver Mystery
> Magazine, the entire Shaver Mystery
> has been taken over from "Amazing
> Stories". It will be our task from
> henceforth to present all phases
> of the mystery.

# READER'S SECTION

Each issue we will publish as many pertinent letters to the Shaver Mystery as space allows. We urge all readers to contribute any facts, personal or otherwise, to help our research.

Dear Mr. Shaver:

You will doubtless recall the first letter of this type that I wrote to you after the club had been formed. It contained the information that a certain section of the Bear Mountain Interstate Park was of such a character as to bear investigation by some of the members of the club in that district that were interested. Well, not that I want to criticize, but rather that I wish to correct an erroneous statement that if observed by anyone who knows the park, would immediately discredit my information. In the editing of my letter to you in the club magazine, an error was made that changed the entire contents of the letter. The area that I described in my letter was given as north and *west* of Lake Tiorati in the said park. Actually the area is north and *east* of Lake Tiorati in the said park. I believe that upon examination you will find that the latter directions are those given in my letter as against the former that were printed in the magazine. In case I am wrong and did give you the mistaken directions by some queer quirk of fate, then I apologize for calling this to your attention, and saying that it was your mistake. Sadly enough I have been unable to continue my investigations this summer because of an out of state job, now that I am back home ill health has forced my investigations to a standstill for the time being. However during the course of the summer my brother has been able to do a little investigating and here is an excerpt from a report that he gave to me.

"We climbed the mountain—the countryside was clear and visibility good—OUTSIDE the area. The trail was grown over for about the first half mile—just enough to discourage prospective hikers. I went on because I wanted to and I'd be darned if I'd let any place stop me twice in a row. After that distance the trail became more distinct and well worn—recently traveled—not just by a few people at long intervals. Then, after a while Paul remarked, "It's awfully quiet, isn't it." Also the lookout points were of no value—the valley was shrouded in mist making the taking of pictures senseless.

I think, that combined with my last letter this should begin to read as a fairly interesting yarn . . . Oliver J. Barton, Jr., 13 Irving Place, Summit, N. J.

*Ok. Correction noted. Very interesting. Hope we hear from CHMBS on it. Shaver.*

Dear Mr. Shaver:

At the time I sent the last letter to you I was on my way to New York City for a week-end visit. On my return, during the recent hot spell, I had two consecutive nights of torment of a form I have never had before. Both nights I experienced all the agony of a prolonged and strong electric shock WHILE LYING ON A CLOTH MATTRESS AND WELL AWAY FROM ANY ELECTRIC LINES OF ANY SORT AND ON A "FAIR" NIGHT WHEN THERE WAS NO EVIDENCE OF LIGHTNING! The next night (third) I suffered a queer pain in my back unlike any I have ever experienced. What the source was I will not attempt to guess.

On the fourth night I, for the first time in my life, heard what may be "dero" voices. At least, a "thought" which seemed more like someone speaking to me and calling me by name made certain suggestions to me which I shall not list here but which were not the type you would call of a "high moral" order. I am not in the habit of thinking in such a way that my thoughts have to be addressed to myself as "Joe"! Nor were the ideas of the order I have ever had—though sex thoughts as such are not at all new to me at this time of life!

O.K. maybe I'm nuts to tell all that I have—probably won't be believed nor considered important.

Swell job on both issues. Make them bigger and better. Don't worry about the art!

J. F. Pearce, 48 Hubbard St., Malden 48, Mass.

*Dear J.F.: Now you know what I mean when I talk about deros. Maybe we are nuts, J.F. but thousands and thousands of others have the same kind of thing happen to them, and I've got the letters to prove it. According to the profs they are all nuts. The Profs are far outnumbered, at least. Maybe we should investigate them? They even believe an astronomer can tell how far away Sirius was on the night of June Eleventh! And that space is curved! Can you curve a space, J.F.? I always thought a curve was two dimensional. Maybe it's a cucumber . . . Shaver*

Dear Mr. Shaver:

This is a rather belated letter of appreciation. I think your magazine is something super-special. Of course, anything in science-fiction or fantasy is my meat; but, all arguments about truth or fiction aside, Shaver stories are in a class by themselves—right up at the top.

I don't know if there is anything in my experience that would be of interest to you or help your investigations but it won't hurt to talk about them. I have always been a day dreamer—nothing odd about that, but some of my dreams come true!

Take a trip through a B-17; take a look at the maze of wires and tubing, radio, radar, gun turrets, and instruments. It was very strange and amazing the first time I saw it. Yet it all seemed strangely familiar as if I had seen a lot of that sort of thing before.

I have dreamed of things like television before I knew it existed. Yes, I even imagined a gadget like your all-seeing-eye ray mech. Ten years before you wrote about it. Maybe it is not unusual for a person to look at present day civilization and see the shape of things to come, but I was raised on a farm a long way from the nearest city and saw practically nothing of civilization.

I have long had the impression I was born in the wrong century, or to put it more accurately, that I did not "belong" in the environment I found myself in. I think my strangest experience was to find part of my consciousness standing aloof and criticizing my actions as being foolish. Rather as if my mind was a separate entity from the body it inhabits. Could it be I mistook some one else's thought for my own? If that is the case the other mind has become a part of me over the years.

It always makes me feel terribly lonely to think that the minds of my friends are a closed book to me. I somehow feel that I should "know" their thoughts, without having to interpret their words and actions. Sometimes I am pleasantly surprised to find I do know just how they feel and what they are thinking but that is very seldom. Less pleasant is my ability to feel strong emotions in others. I once saw a French mob go after a traitor. It was very distasteful but for a moment I could have killed the man as cheerfully as any of them.

The theory today of all sin and evil in the world today being caused by sun poisons is a very interesting one. There is a lot of cancer in this part of the country. Maybe it is because at this altitude there is less air to shield men from the sun's rays. The steady stream of destructive rays from such a clear open sky would cause body cells to mutate and "grow wild". However I think life is tenacious enough to adapt itself to almost all conditions. Would it not be possible for healthy life to thrive on "de"? After all energy can be converted from one type to another. I rather suspect that de and the atomic energy we are familiar with are quite feeble compared to the "integrate" life energies. There is no end to the number of possibilities.

Speaking of mutations, the stories written about them irk me even if they are only fiction. Freaks and super-men-bah! Neither has a good chance of survival in this world. A favorable mutation with a high survival value would look the same as anyone else. Chances are he wouldn't know he was different or realize his powers, but over a few thousand years homo sapiens would be replaced by homo superior and no one would be the wiser. Men would only wonder that the world had become so much more pleasant and that they had advanced so far beyond their ancestors.

Incidentally I want to remark that I hope all your stories can be proven true and that we can save some of the wonders of the Elder Race for our upper world. If I can be of any help—, I'd go to hell and back just for the ride . . . L. L. Layton, W.E.E. R.C.A.F., Edmonton, Alberta.

*Dear Mr. L. L. Layton:*

*So you wish you could know the minds of your friends. You could, if it wasn't for the repressive secrecy around the existence of the telaug, it would be as casual a part of our life ar radio. And vastly more useful. There wouldn't be any crime, because a criminal couldn't plan one without people knowing. He would carry crime around in his mind like a striped suit on a prisoner. Maybe that's why it's secret. Cross out the maybe.*

*Life can't adapt to de any more than wood can adapt to fire. Life does thrive on the products of de, just as plants thrive on wood ashes.*

*The integrate life energies are the important side of energy. They are untouched as such by science, the very concept of their existence is almost unspoken of by scientific writers. It is the great unknown of research, integration is a little used word. Disintegration, the enemy of life, that they know and use. But do not mention integration, the concept is not accepted as a necessary concomitant of theoretical wool, today. I wonder where they think the word came from? . . . Shaver*

*PS. The proofs prepared for publication in April issue of AS have been ordered not to be published . . .*

Dear Mr. Shaver:

In the first issues of your Mystery Magazine you stressed the fact that they (the Tero) needed us and our help. A possible solution to the problem popped into my head, so here it is:

Let the Club form a company and all who are interested can buy shares at say one dollar each. Then, since you are acquainted with some of the Tero, you be a purchasing agent and acquire such of their machines as you can, especially the healing types. The medium of exchange can be money or produce or merchandise, whichever they need most.

After a machine is ours, it can be analyzed and studied and blue prints made. The company can then manufacture many and the profits will enable you to purchase other types.

On page 30 of Volume II Jas. R. Guyton Jr., mentions the Chinese as coming from the Moon, and it started a train of thought in my mind.

Back around 1930, a friend who is a strong medium and I held seances. One result was the Mound builder alphabet which I sent you last year. We asked questions of a man named Blue Moon, who had been an early chief, and he told of having come from a sun, landing at what is known as Buffalo, N. Y. and spreading out from there.

They were not very warlike, and could not repulse their later enemies, the Indians, who finally drove them out. I've regretted since that day I didn't ask where they migrated to.

Regarding the Mound Builders, Blue Moon said they had a yellow complexion with reddish hair.

Some years ago, about 11 miles N.E. of here, on the Maple Island Road, a construction gang opened a mound, and one skull had some red hair still matted to the bone, according to one of the men, Angus Orcutt, whom I know slightly . . . Percy L. Mann, 428 McLaughlin, Muskegon, Mich.

*Percy Mann:*

*The trouble with buying some of those mech is the monopoly has the price set up around fifty thousand. Not only that, after they get a sucker to pay, the machine disappears from his home, safe, or what have you shortly thereafter. When he squalks, he finds people consider him nuts for mentioning what happened.*

*Tain't true, fella, tain't true. Where'd you ever get such crazy ideas?*

*Plenty of rich people aren't as rich as they used to be, I've heard. But of course it's only a hoax, so don't believe a word I say.*

*I always wondered about the mound builders, once read a volume about them too big to lift. I propped it up on the floor, read it lying down. It weighed as much as I did. I was ten.*

*So they had red hair and yellow skins. That book never said a word about that! But they sure made a lot of darn funny looking pottery. Those naughty mound builders. I think the philistines killed them for being lewd . . . Shaver*

Dear Mr. Shaver:

Just received your latest book on the Thought Records. I am sending you a thought that a friend dictated to me a few years ago. It was very strange as to the way it came to him. We were sitting in my home one evening and suddenly he said to me, "Get a paper and pencil, I have something to say." Well, here it is.

"Give up earth. Stop this ceaseless and useless spatting and pumet into the eternity of space that surrounds you, and thus save your millions and millions of beligerent peoples who have nothing more or less to do than to fight, to quarrel, and to kill. You are so full of rust, rot and decay that I am nauseated half to death by the reeking stink and smell. Everywhere are the cries of the uncared for sick, the shrieks of the dying, and the bickering of the almighty rich, and the wailing of the lonely poor.

Everywhere everything is tarnished and blemished beyond recognition by floods, famine, wars, and every other god forsaked calamity that can befall one people.

I ask myself why humans cannot live as humans, happy and content with each other's company. Still one man kills the other for what he has and is killed for what he possesses.

Give up your God forsaken earth for you are beaten."

I never thought much of the above until I read of your mystery. Just the other day I asked him why he had asked me to write it down for him. He said he didn't know. While he was giving me the thought his eyes seemed to be worlds away. Thanks very much for taking the time for reading this . . . Henry West, 138 Lincoln Street, Midvale, Utah.

*Dear Henry West:*

*Only a man from another and better planet would have made your friend dictate those words. It is just one more evidence that the caves are visited by extra-terrestrials . . . Shaver*

Dear Mr. Shaver:

It is only natural that I should say that I hope the Shaver Mystery Magazine will stick to its magnificently broad and liberal policy as expressed in the editorial. Many magazines, as you know, do slowly change, through politics or change of editors, etc., and heaven knows what. Sticking to your policy, you will need and deserve a government appropriation, Roosevelt style, which is just the reason you will not get it, but help you will get.

I have several interested parties here. One, Professor Schwartz, is a man of about 45 years, who too has made a long study of the cave problem, beginning when he was 15 years old in Germany.

As you know, the literature on the cave problem is quite extensive now. Even before the war, the Germans too, privately and perhaps governmentally, were considering it. Caves are extremely useful militarily now, with bombing raids what they are. Prof. Schwartz says that a Nazi-Gestapo man was here before the last war, seeking entrances to the reputed Peru and Mt. Shasta tunnels, and seeking to compel Prof. Schwartz to cooperate although Prof. Schwartz is not a Nazi, nor ever was one, so far as I know.

In the first place, any good book about Yucatan and the Mayas will inform you that the entire peninsula is honey-combed "with natural limestone caves and underground rivers". The two, as you know, quite naturally go together often.

But, and second, these are not the caves in question. We are speaking of caves in granitic sections, which give evidence of nature having been improved upon by man, or of being entirely man-made.

Prof. Schwartz says that a Nazi of the Gestapo came upon an enormous circular pit. Its sides dropped vertically for 300 meters. (1000 feet, or as much as the Empire State Building). Trees could be seen growing tall and straight below. Eagles soared around, and then dived to the center of the bottom, apparently to eat something. Since the sides were dangerously steep, the Nazi had to content himself with his binoculars.

Returning with others, he eventually discovered a similar but much narrower bore, or shaft, not far from the first, which is so big that it cannot be hidden in any way. Not having cable or apparatus with which to let down a man in the seemingly bottomless shaft, they let down pencil and paper. To their surprise, the cord, when drawn back up, was found to be cut clean, as with a knife, or scissors. And no pencil or paper. Of course they all resolved to come back for serious work, but the war cut them off from that too. All this was in Guatemala, north Quezaltenango, which is high in the mountains, apart.

Near the above place is a witch doctor, friendly to Prof. Schwartz. The doctor assured the professor that there is a secret passage, closed by a revolving rock door, which goes to the still enormous chamber which is still below the enormous roof cave-in, seen from above. Nothing was said about deros, or the purpose of the chamber of tunnels, or their length or direction. Probably the witch doctor doesn't dare explore very much.

Prof. Schwartz believes that he could take us to the place. It is not too inaccessible. He even mentioned inviting you and the others with you so that we could all go and do a thorough job. Prof. Schwartz life-long desire has been to explore these caves or tunnels. I have confirmed this from others who know him. Naturally he was very happy to find one who goes without coaxing.

But the Nazi too was interested, too interested. He even tried to compel Prof. Schwartz to accompany him. Regarding the information, beliefs, hopes, and intentions of the Nazi, you can guess with the same probability of certainty as I. For me the above is true enough as far as it goes, and as far as I can ascertain to date, without alienating anybody, or going personally to explore, as I am trying to do . . . waiting vacations.

I am as sorry as you that at present I can only exchange tantalizingly incomplete mysteries between us. To others, they get us nowhere, apparently, and only cost expensive explorations. I know other aggravating mysteries of the same class . . . incomplete. Professor W. Wiers, Azueta No. 32, Mexico, D.F.

*Dear friend Professor Wiers:*

*The Mayan glyphs seem to me to tell a story of Mayan discoveries in the caverns. Other sources have told me of Mayan work and Mayan connections with the caverns. There are ancient Spanish books which tell the same story, of Spanish discoveries during the conquest and later.*

*I am hoping we do get help such as you mention.*

*Mr. Schwartz' experience is very interesting to me. We have in our files many letters of a similar kind, of various parts of the wor'd. I wish we had resources to pursue all these leads to their ultimate revelation . . . Shaver*

Dear Mr. Shaver:

From your stories in Amazing and now in the Shaver Mystery Magazine, I gather that the Atlans and Titans lived about the same time the early dinosaurs were roaming the earth. Supposedly, there was no radio-activity in the air from the sun and the Atlans and the titans were still living on the earth's surface. That could account for the fact that the reptiles grew to such immense size. Just how did they get along with the dinosaurs on the earth's surface? Perhaps they built their cities with a wall of force shielding them, and built underground roadways to connect them. Then they left the reptiles to their jungle domains, or killed them all off for food, or made pets out of them for all I know. What did happen?

Did the Atlans and Titans build their caves before or after the ice age? If their cities were built before, they would have been buried and killed, unless they foresaw that and had the time to transfer everything underground. Of course I should take under consideration that the ice flows moved slowly enough for them to get away.

I cannot understand why you are so interesting in investigating all of the claims from readers of cave entrance locations. Since you have already been there yourself, you ought to know the safest means of entering the caves. If the deros have the powerful machines that you say they do, they certainly know that you are trying to expose them, and will do everything in their power to stop you from exposing them. Don't get the idea that I do not believe your statements on their tremendous machines, but it is impossible for me or anyone to truly believe you that hasn't seen them with their own eyes. I don't think that they will allow you to gather any really incriminating evidence on them if they have the means to dispose of people as you write about. That is unless you lead a charmed life.

Perhaps you have answered these questions at an earlier date in your writing, but if so I haven't seen them . . . Jack Hart, 404 Linden, Birmingham, Michigan.

*Dear Jack Hart,*

*As I get it the dinos appeared on earth after the Elder race left, though they had some giant reptiles, perhaps as exhibits. They had brought a lot of different life forms here from other planets. Under them, the whole planet was a cultivated garden forest, one gigantic farm, the caverns underneath their homes. The jungle days came after, in the days of the latter Gods. The Latter Gods were widely separated, few and pretty savage in nature.*

*Some caves were built before earth was anything but a cold dark planet. Others after they had a beneficial sun. Few after the sun aged and become the source of age.*

*Flames from the sun seem to have swept over earth at one time, floods because of near approach of the moon or other bodies, several times. Thus all traces of their surface structures have vanished except those called the Cyclopean ruins. These are of several types; Greek classic time temples were erected on such ruins.*

*You are right they won't let me gather much evidence, the proofs we had prepared for publication have been stopped from publication. No more Shaver Mystery in Amazing. That doesn't make it any easier to believe me, does it. I didn't expect anyone to believe me who had no contact with rays, but such people alone make a large audience.*

*The deros would be vastly more powerful than they are, but evil itself is a stupidty, they are not too smart.*

*I want this information about entrances because I want to get back in, the one I entered is no longer anything but a death trap.*

*The ice age was an aftermath of the moon approach, as I get it. Anybody's guess is as good as mine on subjects, and no better, I assure you. There were at least two ice ages, and several world floods.*

*The period of warmth after the first sun on earth was very short. It was a period of intense growth of which the Elder race took full advantage, left immediately the sun began to throw heavier metals . . . Shaver*

Dear Mr. Shaver:

I've read all your stories since the first and have been impressed with the same. My mother has always claimed to be very psychic, so after reading the first story I tried a trick on her. I know for a fact that she had never even heard of Amazing Stories so she could not have known about the story. So one day while we were doing the dishes I just turned to her and asked her casually what she knew about the Cave people. She looked stunned and asked me why I asked such a question. I told her to please answer my question first and here's what she told me.

She said she had a dream vision and that the cave people had shown her the marvelous machinery that was in the caves. She described some of them and they corresponded with your description of them. Mind you, she had never heard of you or your mystery. I then told her about it and not long after she called me on the telephone and told me about the deros in Mexico and it corresponded with what later came out in the readers discussion in Amazing Stories.

There has been a cave discovered here in California or Nevada with the remains of mummies eight and nine feet tall but it has been hushed up for some reason. Very little was said about it. I wonder why?

Well I hope you keep publishing the magazine and I'm one that's going to keep taking it . . . Gladys Rowland, 3031 Victoria Ave., Los Angeles 16, Calif.

*Dear Gladys Rowland:*

*I hope we keep on publishing too. I wonder too why they hush up these discoveries. Look what they did with the flying saucers. We still get letters from people who see them. We even got samples of materials from exploding discs. But not a whisper in the papers. Even if it was an illusion, they ought to let us have our fun with them, eh? Unfortunately, they are real, and we aren't to believe it. Somehow, I wonder what they do believe in. Santa Claus is bad for Children, dear. He's a fairy.*

*Wish you could hear the voice records we have from investigators of flying saucer eye witnesses. And read the letter files . . . Shaver*

Dear Mr. Shaver:

You are doing a beautiful job on the Shaver Mystery Club. Your cover designs are absolutely priceless and without them the way they are, the magazine wouldn't be the Shaver Mystery Club. Keep them up.

I noticed in the second issue that some man by the name Thomas A. Smith, feels abused at feasting his eyes at such a beautiful work of art. If his mind is so full of "De" that he cannot appreciate the perfect work of a truly great artist, because the subject in the nude happened to be that of the one thing that makes life worth living on any planet and in any language, that of the female of the specie, without thinking lewd thoughts that he even objected to them himself, then he is either too young to be reading your exceptionally fine magazine or else he is the type of man who looks at a beautiful pair of legs walking along the street and then lets his mind get so far out of normal self control that he goes home, gets down on his knees and prays to some Being for forgiveness. I would suggest that he stick to the Sunday School Times, or the Christian Herald, for his reading.

Your covers are masterpieces of art and the man who drew them sure knows his stuff. He evidently studied the human body because no ignoramus could draw with such perfection, and attention to detail.

Smith doesn't consider the human body and the study of it, to be at all scientific but is it not written, "The greatest study of mankind is man"? When a race of men live on and on for hundreds and thousands of years, it is to be expected that they know so much about the human body that the appearance of a beautiful woman in the nude would be given no unusual notice nor would they go home and hide their heads in shame. Only when they set their minds to the delights of the pursuit of a fair female would their blood pressure mount above normal. Why be ashamed of the human body, clothed or naked, when it is the greatest mech in the world; even greater than any of the cavern mech.

The minute you make up your minds to produce cover pictures of the bees and trees and etc., then return the unused balance of my subscription money to me and cancel future copies of the Shaver Mystery Club . . . Charles P. Glover, 51 First Place, Broadalbin, N. Y.

*Dear Charles:*

*The guy that did Ardala on the cover is named Malcolm Smith, too. Thomas and Malcolm should have a heart to heart talk, methinks. Maybe they could get together on how a picture should be looked at. Malcolm is a very interesting man to meet.*

*The Elder race considered it a sin to deprive anyone of anything that didn't hurt. Only ugly people worried about others seeing them. But we do live in "modern" times, and it seems that moderns have ideas somewhat different. Like no shorts on Main street. With a Jantzen poster in every haberdashery . . . oh, well. It's a world of contradictions. Don't you say anything, or write anything, or think anything I don't approve of I'll have you stopped. That's organized stfanism, I have learned. You be a Shaver fan, not a stfan . . . Shaver*

---

## AN IMPORTANT ANNOUNCEMENT !

As you all know, the SHAVER MYSTERY MAGAZINE has been anything but on a regular publishing schedule- up until now. But with this issue we are going to adopt a regular bi-monthly schedule, and adhere to it. Our printing problems have been great, but finally we have managed to overcome them. And together with the fact that from this issue on, as announced on page 18 of this issue, the SHAVER MYSTERY CLUB has taken over the entire SHAVER MYSTERY from "AMAZING STORIES" as announced in that magazine. The reason being that positive proof is now available as to the truth of the mystery, and since we can no longer guise it as fiction AMAZING STORIES is turning over the proof to your club magazine. It will be our duty to present you with all available evidence from this day forward, a task that your editor has already made his life's work and which will, he hopes, be the answer to many of the great mysteries science has been unable to answer except with casual shrugs... To this end are we dedicated.

# The Mystery of the Flying Disks

## . . . A Proof of the Shaver Mystery . . .

Published in cooperation with FATE MAGAZINE on sale in February at all newsstands

ON JUNE 24, 1947, Kenneth Arnold, a flying Boise, Idaho businessman, saw weird disks flying through the air at better than 1000 miles per hour. Within a week the world was goggle-eyed. The newspapers made headlines out of it for ten days, but two weeks later, Kenneth Arnold and all others who claimed to have seen the flying mysteries were labeled irresponsible crackpots by official sources. On July 10 "flying saucer" stories stopped appearing in the newspapers as though they had been censored.

*Had* they been censored? If so, why, how and by whom?

On July 4, Coast Guard Yeoman Frank Ryman took a picture of a flying disk or disks, which showed four white dots, three of which were claimed to be flaws in the negative, the fourth seeming to be authentic. But with such doubtful evidence, nothing could be proved.

Show us some *pictures!* demanded the big dailies.

On July 7, William H. Rhodes of Phoenix, Arizona, snapped two pictures of a flying disk circling over the city. He turned these pictures over to *The Arizona Republic,* Phoenix newspaper, which published them on page one of the July 9 edition. These pictures were not merely dots in a negative, but showed the definite shape of the flying disks, and revealed that they had a hole or a bright spot in their centers. There were a great many witnesses, some of whom later said when asked, that the photos were reproductions of the objects they had seen in the skies.

Here was *proof positive* that these objects were not just "spots before the eyes," but actually flying disks of an aeronautical design unrecognizable by experts.

Those pictures never reached any other newspapers! Why? They were the *hottest* news in the world on July 9! On July 10 complete silence descended over the "flying saucer" story.

Was it because the flying disks were a military secret?

We asked aviation expert John C. Ross about this. Elsewhere in this magazine you will find his answer under the title "What Were The Flying Doughnuts?" in which he gives his reasons why the disks are not a military project.

Based on information we present here, Kenneth Arnold, of Boise, Idaho is a highly competent observer, and he did see these objects and correctly charted their course and speed. His story is also in this magazine, under the title "I *Did* See the Flying Disks!"

The following is a quotation of the story published under the by-line of Robert C. Hanika in *The Arizona Republic* for July 9:

*Speedy "Saucer" Zips Through Local Sky*

The first clearly recorded photographs of what is believed to be a mysterious "flying disk" which has 33 states in America and even a few foreign countries on edge with its peculiar activities, was taken by an amateur Phoenix photographer.

Reproduced in *The Arizona Republic* today, the photographs were made by William A. Rhodes, 4333 North 14th Street, who was on his way to his workshop in the rear of his home when he heard the distinctive "whoosh" of what he believed to be a P-80 or Shooting Star jet-propelled plane.

Rhodes snatched a camera from his workshop bench, and by the time he reached a small mound at the rear of his home, the object was banking in tight circles to the south at approximately 1,000 feet, he said.

In the overcast sky the object continued its speedy flight from north to south and directly east of his stance. Rhodes snapped the hurtling missile by sighting alongside his box camera.

Quickly rolling up his last piece of film, Rhodes awaited the return of the craft which continued in a clockwise movement over his home, and as it disappeared into the west the second shot was taken.

Rhodes described the object's disappearance as phenomenal since it apparently winged over and shot up into the ether.

"I don't think it was a P-80, since I have observed many of them over here. Also, the fact that it made no other sound after the first pass over the house," Rhodes said, "makes me believe it was some other type of aircraft. In its three flights over the house there was not a sound, even when it zoomed into the southwest," he said.

Men long experienced in aircraft recognition studied the prints and the negatives from which they were made, and declined to make guesses on what the flying object might be.

Rhodes' first shot was made as the object approached, and showed it to be somewhat cigar-shaped, but with motion-lines on the film which indicated it was turning at high speed, either edgewise or in a flat spin.

The second, as the object "banked" in a tight turn, showed an object much the shape of a heel of a shoe, with a small hole in the center. The white mark also showed in the first picture.

Rhodes said there were twin tails of vapor trailing from the points or edges of the rear of the "heel."

A print of photograph number two is reproduced with this article and a drawing, taken from the cut on page one of *The Arizona Republic* is also reproduced, showing photo number one. Photo number one also included a skyline of trees and a telephone wire, adding to its authenticity.

On August 2, *The Tacoma Times* published the following story under the by-line of Paul Lantz:

*Sabotage Hinted in Crash of*
*Army Bomber At Kelso*

The mystery of the "Flying Saucers" soared into prominence again Saturday when *The Tacoma Times* was informed that the crash Friday of an army plane at Kelso may have been caused by sabotage.

The Times' informant, in a series of mysterious phone calls, reported that the ship had been sabotaged "or shot down" to prevent shipment of flying disk fragments to Hamilton field, Cal., for analysis.

The disk parts were said by the informant to be those from one of the mysterious platters which plunged to earth on Maury island recently.

Lending substance to the caller's story is the fact that 12 HOURS BEFORE THE ARMY RELEASED OFFICIAL INDENTIFICATION, he correctly indentified the dead in the crash to be Capt. William L. Davidson, pilot, and First Lt. Frank M. Brown.

At the same time he informed The Times Kenneth Arnold, Boise businessman who first sighted the flying saucers, and United Airlines Capt. E. J. Smith, who also sighted them, were in secret conference in Room 502 of the Hotel Winthrop. A check confirmed the information, but neither Smith nor Arnold would disclose the nature of the conference nor the reason for their being in Tacoma.

According to the anonymous caller, platter fragments were loaded aboard a B-25 at McChord field Friday for shipment to the California field. Half an hour after the take off, the plane crashed. near Kelso,

Wash. Two enlisted men, Master Sgt. Elmer L. Taff and Technician Fourth Grade Woodrow D. Mathews parachuted to safety.

At McChord field, an intelligence officer confirmed the mystery caller's report that the ill-fated craft had been carrying "classified material."

Major George Sander explained: "Classified material means there was a somewhat secret cargo aboard the plane. No one was allowed to take pictures of the wreckage until the material was removed and returned to McChord field."

He declined to say what constituted the "Classified material."

The theory of sabotage was borne out by the statement of the two crash survivors that one of the engines burst into flames and that regular fire apparatus installed in the engine for such emergencies failed to function.

Notified of the information passed along by the anonymous informant, Captain Smith said:

"When the story breaks it will be given general release, but it will NOT come from this room."

At the time he was in the Hotel Winthrop in conference with Arnold.

Saturday Smith said he and Arnold would deny anything that was printed about the secret sessions held in the hotel. However, he was visibly disturbed and expressed consternation when notified late Saturday that the names of the dead pilot and co-pilot had been revealed before the army released them.

According to the telephone caller, both the dead officers were members of military intelligence at Hamilton field.

The next significant "flying disk" story comes from page one of the *Sunday Journal* of Portland, Oregon, for Sunday, August 3, 1947. It appeared under the by-line of Larry Howes.

### Kelso Crash, Disks Linked

Two army officers killed Friday in an airplane crash near Kelso, Wash., had visited Portland two days before to question Dick Rankin, noted Northwest flier, about flying disks.

Rankin disclosed this Saturday after a United Press dispatch from Tacoma reported that the plane which carried the men to their deaths had secret cargo aboard. An anonymous informant told United Press that the cargo was fragments of a crashed flying disk.

Rankin said the two officers came to his home, 834 N. E. Simpson street, Wednesday. They questioned him closely four hours about the two flights of mysterious objects he had seen June 14 above Bakersfield, Cal., Rankin said.

Rankin said the two men told him they also had questioned Pilot Kenneth Arnold, Boise, and United Airlines Capt. E. J. Smith, Seattle, who had seen other disk flights.

"They were getting pretty hot on something," said Rankin. "I wouldn't be surprised if something had happened to them."

The two men killed in the crash were identified Saturday by army officials as Capt. William L. Davidson, San Francisco, and Lieut. Frank M. Brown, Vallejo, Cal. Two non-commisioned officers parachuted from the plane before it crashed. One of the survivors said the plane had encountered engine trouble.

"Those two boys who were killed were sitting Wednesday right where you are," Rankin told a *Journal* reporter interviewing him at his home Saturday.

Rankin, brother of the late, famed pioneer Northwest flier, Tex Rankin, uttered the opinion that the disk-like objects are aircraft of a foreign power.

"I've been flying since 1919," he said, "and I've done a lot of mapping. I think whatever country owns them is mapping this country."

Rankin said he told the two now dead army officers of his theory. They neither agreed with nor disputed it, he said.

At Tacoma, Ted Morello, U. P. correspondent, reported he had received anonymous telephone calls saying the ill-fated plane had disk fragments aboard.

Morello said the anonymous informant had "uncannily accurate" information about the crew hours before army officials released the names of the dead.

"In one of a series of calls to United Press yesterday," wrote Morello, "the mystery man identified the dead pilot and co-pilot as 'Capt. Davidson and Lieut. Brown.' Not until hours later did the army make public the names."

The correspondent said the informant also disclosed that Pilot Arnold and Captain Smith were in conference in a Tacoma hotel. The correspondent confirmed the fact by calling the hotel, but was unable to learn what the conference was about.

The United Press writer said an intelligence officer at McChord field Saturday admitted that the ill-fated B-25 carried "classified material."

"That means," Maj. George Sander was quoted, "that there was a somewhat secret cargo aboard. No one was allowed to take pictures of the wreckage until the material had been removed and returned to McChord."

(Reports from the Kelso area indicated that army authorities were searching the wreckage all day for a "little black box.")

The anonymous informant said the plane carried wreckage of a flying disk reported to have crashed last week on Maury island, near Tacoma.

In the Chicago *Sunday Times* for August 3, 1947, appears the following story under the by-line of Maurice Roddy.

*Link "Sky Metal" to Mystery Blast*

A mass of blazing metal reported to have roared down from the sky on an island off the West Coast simultaneously with the recent appearance of "flying saucers" gave a plot last night for an atomic age "Man From Mars" story.

A tragic part of the story lies in the fate of two Army fliers who went to their deaths in the crash of a B-25 bomber while reportedly carrying a load of fragments of the metallic mass.

The mysterious explosion took place June 24 on Maury island off the Washington coast.

A harbor patrol boat in the water nearby was damaged, the captain's son was injured and a dog was killed. (Later information said it was a cat, and that a seagull had been killed. —Ed.)

That blast has been surrounded with the deepest secrecy by Army, Navy and atomic authorities.

. . . described as a "lava oxide metal" . . . the specimens were analyzed by University of Chicago scientists. They identified the stuff as "molten metal which had fallen from great height, landing in sand."

Friday night Capt. (E. J.) Smith attended a conference in Tacoma, Washington. He talked with two B-25 fliers, assigned by the AAF to work exclusively on all reports of "flying saucers" or other phenomena of the sky.

Present at the meeting, too, were Arnold, the Boise pilot, some persons who were aboard the harbor boat damaged off Maury island, and other witnesses.

The conference broke up at 12:30 A.M. and the two Army pilot-investigators took with them a box of specimens, pictures and affidavits from persons who had witnessed the island explosion.

The next thing known of the two B-25 fliers is when their plane crashed. . . .

Whether the box of Maury island "specimen molten lava" aboard the plane had anything to do with the crash has caused considerable speculation.

Authorities at (Hamilton) field admitted the plane had made a flight to McChord field, outside Tacoma, where the conference was held.

They said, too, that the airplane was carrying an "unclassified cargo" and went on to describe it as "hot stuff".

Asked whether the cargo was connected with the Maury island matter, a spokesman at the field said the query was "very close" to the situation.

The next newspaper account which appeared in this connection comes from a U. P. account datelined San Rafael, Calif., August 9.

*It's Official; There Is No Flying Disk*

The Fourth Air Force's long-heralded "report on the flying saucers" came out today.

It decided there were no such things.

Said a report from Lt. Col. Donald L. Springer, intelligence officer and assistant chief of staff of the command:

"There is not sufficient evidence nor testimony available to conclude whether the reports of the so-called flying disks in the Tacoma (Wash.) area or any other area have any basis in fact. In view of this, Fourth Air Force will pursue this particular investigation no further."

Springer brought back from his investigation of the Tacoma area some fragments resembling molten metal, found on Maury island beach.

"Similar material appears in great quantity in that area and in other Tacoma areas," he said, referring to reports that the fused rocks were remnants of 'flying disks'."

He said there was no trace of a box of similar material reportedly aboard a plane that crashed near Kelso, Wash., killing two officers also investigating "disk" reports.

But on November 23 the flying disks were again in the news. Said Dave Johnson, aviation editor of the Boise, Idaho *Statesman,* in the Sunday edition of that paper:

One of the greatest aeronautical mysteries of all time—that of the flying disks—has come to life again. Objects which were reported seen by thousands of persons on the ground, and by scores of pilots in the air, have been sighted off the Pacific coast.

The oceanic appearance of flying disks was the subject of a message transmitted to naval intelligence in San Diego, San Francisco and Seattle. The report also was relayed to the U. S. hydrographic office in San Francisco.

It originated with the second officer of the tanker S.S. Ticonderoga. The tanker was at a position 300 miles north of San Francisco, and 25 miles off the coast on Nov. 12 when the officer reported that he saw two flying disks.

This is the report:

"Two flying disks were sighted flying southwest at high speed. They appeared about 36 feet in diameter and were 20 feet apart. They emitted a very bright glow and left a streak about 50 feet behind them. They were first sighted bearing west at 0620 Greenwich central time. The fix (position of the vessel) was latitude 43 degrees 15 minutes north and 124 degrees 54 minutes west."

It is the first time that the objects reported in such profusion during the months have been observed after the hours of darkness as emitting a glow and a trail.

Airline pilots who sighted the objects over Idaho during the months of July and September saw nothing that would indicate any light associated with the disks.

After receiving the report that disks had been sighted at sea, we telephoned an intelligence officer assigned to one of the air forces in the United States. This air force had received "orders from the top" to expend every effort in tracking down the possible source of flying disks.

We cannot give this officer's name. But, he said he is now convinced that something as far as he understands, has been flying over the United States, and the source of that something is not known either to the Army or the Navy.

We have also learned that the Army has asked what it considers its most creditable witnesses of flying disks to draw pictures of what they saw. These drawings have all been generally the same.

These sketches are of an object with a rounded nose and a tail with a sharp point, much like a tadpole. As far as is publicly known, nobody has been able to get a clear photograph of the objects, although many people tried.

The Army has a number of photographs. We have two of them. We are told that the Army considers them to be "reliable" photographs. We have not seen the original negatives. The pictures show the objects to resemble the structure we have come to associate with supersonic aircraft. The front portion resembles a flying wing. In the center of both photographs is a dot of light. We don't know what it is. It could be either a hole or a glassed-in dome creating a reflection.

The officer with whom we talked appeared extremely interested in the blue light which glared over a 250-mile area of southern Idaho and eastern Oregon a few weeks ago. He said he was not convinced it was a meteoric display. Three men, two United Airlines pilots and a CAA air carrier inspector riding with them, observed this light from a point near Baker, Oregon. They said that after the light expired there was a trail of luminescent particles in the air which slowly assumed an arc of 180 degrees and vanished.

This information is passed on with an objective point of view. We draw no conclusions. The question still remains: What are, or what were, the flying disks?

The following U. P. story dated November 24, originating in San Francisco, is significant in the light of the Ticonderoga incident, and may very well be an important contribution to the solution of the mystery of the flying disks, although it does not seem, from a casual viewpoint, to concern itself with those aerial objects:

*Navy Clips 'Phantom" Reef Yarn*

The Navy today had officially denied the existence of a mysterious undersea mountain reported looming under the shipping lanes to San Francisco, but puzzled crew members of Navy survey ships still were wondering if they had discovered a "phantom reef" 400 miles off the California coast.

The "reef" was "seen" by the crews of several ships who reported "a large mass" under the water off the Golden Gate.

But the Navy ocean survey ship Maury and three smaller vessels sent out to investigate the story said they could find no mountain, shoal—or anything—at the position given in two separate reports.

Capt. F. D. Hambling, skipper of the Maury, admitted his crew was wondering, however, if there still might not be something the survey had missed.

"We received one indication on our echo sounding gear," Capt. Hambling said. "When we were within a mile of the reported location of the shoal, we picked up an echo from a mass about 1,600 yards to one side.

"We changed course and started toward it, proceeding slowly. When we were about 400 yards from the object, it disappeared, and we didn't get another echo. We tracked and retracked the area, using our fathometers and sounding gear—covered about five miles square carefully, and another five miles around the outside of that area."

It is quite evident from the material we have presented that the "story" of the flying disks is not fictional, psychological, spots before the eyes, a delusion or beer bottle caps. It is also evident that military authorities in this country are quite concerned about the flying disks, and equally in the dark concerning their identity, their base or bases, and the possibility of an unfriendly attitude on the part of the disks.

The unfriendliness is suggested by the mysterious informant who claimed in one of his telephone calls to the newspapers that the B-25 carrying Davidson and Brown was "shot down", and by the copyrighted story by David Shapiro, writer for the North American Newspaper Alliance, Inc., telling of two new Nazi weapons invented in Franco Spain which it was suggested might be responsible for the "flying saucer" visions and also for one or two airplane accidents in this country. Thus, there seems to be good reason to suspect that some of the unexplained air crashes could have been "shot down" after all. The very fact that this suspicion exists, and that the flying saucers also exist as proved by photographic and competent observation, would seem to indicate that our protective forces are concerned over the matter.

The evidence uncovered by the editors of this magazine prove that Army and Navy and Air Force Intelligence has been seriously handicapped by the fiasco that resulted from newspaper publicity of the "flying saucers." The matter, a very serious one, and requiring a great amount of cooperation between civilians who observed the saucers and military intelligence, became a laughing stock, and such men as Kenneth Arnold and Capt. E. J. Smith became very reluctant to discuss their observations with anyone, especially intelligence officers, who must be coldly skeptical and thorough in their investigations.

The net result of the nation-wide newspaper debacle was a closing down of thousands of possible sources of vital information. Faced with this, it is no wonder that responsible parties in Intelligence refused to make comments, or tried their level best to suppress the matter by statements such as was made by Lt. Colonel Springer. Lt. Colonel Springer is a member of 4th Air Force Intelligence, and one of the smartest men in the Service. We can sympathize with his job, and we can fully understand the necessity of squelching the saucer "scare" by issuing an official denial which might leave him open to future ridicule if and when the flying saucers proved to be a reality.

The purpose of this article is to aid in reestablishing contact between such men as he and the civilian observers who are now keeping quiet for fear of ridicule or even worse. Such observers are urged to provide military intelligence with detailed information of their observations, which will be held strictly confidential, and which will not result in exposure to ridicule or persecution.

Strange aircraft, then, called variously flying disks, saucers and globes, have been, and still are, flying over this country, and also in other parts of the world. Primarily they seem to be of three types—the saucer-shaped craft Kenneth Arnold saw, approximately as large as our largest transport planes, smaller craft, ranging from three feet in diameter (remotely controlled?) to fifty feet in diameter, and giant golden-colored spheres up to a mile in diameter which fly only at tremendous altitudes.

On at least two occasions, these craft have either crashed or suffered accidents, so that material from them could be gathered. One of these accidents occurred over Maury Island, Washington, and the other near Zamalayuca in Mexico. Both were thoroughly investigated by military intelligence. Material picked up on the scene of the Maury Island accident has been analyzed.

The analysis is as follows:

*High Constituents*—Calcium, Iron, Zinc, Titanium.

*Middle Constituents*—Aluminum, Manganese, Copper, Magnesium, Silicon.

*Low Constituents*—Nickel, Lead, Strontium, Chromium.

*Traces*—Silver, Tin, Cadmium.

Nothing of an unusual nature exists in this combination of metals except the unusually high quantity of calcium. Calcium oxidizes when heated, and its presence in high-constituent quantity in a fused metal which has been subjected to extreme heat is highly unlikely. Technically, it would involve a very difficult processing procedure. Its presence in this material is mystifying. If it is a manufactured substance, its purpose in the mixture is equally difficult to understand.

Two Army Air Force Intelligence officers, engaged in a very serious investigation of flying disk stories, considered this substance of importance, and lost their lives in securing it. Further, there are circumstances in the crash in which they died that do not lend themselves readily to the theory that it was entirely an accident.

It is quite definite that a large box of these fragments were loaded aboard that plane, and it is also quite definite that no trace of them was found in the wreckage. However, in as complete a crash as this one obviously was, very little remains of the plane itself, much less of its cargo. Yet, in a thorough search, at least a few of the fragments should reasonably have been recovered. According to the stories of the two men who parachuted to safety, the intelligence men also had sufficient time to save themselves. It can be assumed that they considered disposal of their secret cargo even more important than their lives. Did they die because they stayed to jettison the mysterious fragments? What did they know, not known today, which made such an act necessary?

There is no likely place for such gigantic ships as are indicated by many observers, except that pointed out by the observation of flying disks off San Francisco, and the simultaneous observation from three separate ships of a "new reef" at the same spot where no reef had been. The Navy investigated this "reef" and announced it did not exist—although the men who made the search are not so sure, having actually recorded a large underwater obstruction while approaching from a distance of 1600 feet to within 400 feet, when it suddenly ceased registering.

Here, then, we have a quite logical base for strange craft—the ocean. Giant "flying boats" could hide beneath the surface, and travel as submarines, emerging to take to the air when necessary, or serve as launching platforms for smaller "disks". There is more than a little evidence to support such a theory; there are dozens of records of weird "wheels" seen underwater by seafaring men.

But what real proof have we, beyond the photos taken at various places, and the sworn statements of many witnesses? There is the very questionable item of the "lava rock" picked up on Maury Island. Here is the story of that single incident, as related by Kenneth Arnold, who, resenting the adverse publicity he received on his own account of flying disks, went to Tacoma, Washington, himself to investigate the reports of the members of the Harbor Patrol who reported six flying disks and produced fragments they said fell from one of them:

The following account (says Mr. Arnold) is what actually took place between the dates of July 28 and August 3, 1947 concerning my investigations of a flying disk at Tacoma, Washington:

Prior to July 28 I had received information of a Mr. Harold A. Dahl and a Mr. Fred L. Crisman of the Harbor Patrol at Tacoma, who had experienced something strange and had fragments of what they thought could be a flying disk. At the noon luncheon of the Advertising Club in Boise, Idaho, I was asked to recount my original observation of flying disks. I mentioned what I'd heard concerning the men in Tacoma, and Mr. Mathews, one of the members, told me after the luncheon that he knew Mr. Dahl personally, knew that he was reliable, and had worked with him for several years on the Harbor Patrol. Until then I had not put any real credence into the report.

I discussed whether I should investigate this affair with Dave Johnson, aviation editor of the Boise *Statesman*. Dave Johnson also observed some of these flying disks, and I put great stock in his advice. He told me it might be worth-while.

It was July 30 at dawn I took off in my own plane, intending to reach Tacoma before dark and contact Mr. Dahl.

It was at 7:00 o'clock that morning I sighted a formation of small disks going south at 4,000 feet as I was letting down at LaGrande, Oregon. I attempted to turn and catch up with them, but they were out of sight before I could complete my turn. I did have my camera on them all the time these objects were in my vision. I would judge them about 30 inches across, very thin, and light brown in color. My movie try was not very successful as there were some 25 objects in this flight and my film only recorded one or two, and these could be seen only under a jeweler's glass.

That afternoon I flew over almost the same route I had flown the day I first observed the flying disks.

It was dusk when I landed at Barry's Airport, which is a little airport located down on the mud flats. I am sure neither Barry nor his wife recognized me as the man whose picture had been in the paper connected with flying disk stories. Here I had my plane gassed and tied up for the night and called a number of hotels trying to get a room for the night. I was unable to find a room until I called the Winthrop Hotel, the largest and most prominent hotel in the City of Tacoma. To my surprise, they had a room with bath for me, called me by name, and seemed to be expecting me.

I went directly to the hotel and while preparing to take a bath, called Mr. Dahl. I told him who I was, why I had come to Tacoma, and said:

"I understand, Mr. Dahl, you have refused to talk or discuss the matter of the flying disks with any of the newspapers; or with anyone, for that matter. There are various aspects to your story that lead me to believe you have experienced something that is real and whether it is for publication or whether it is not, for my personal satisfaction, I would like to hear your story."

He told me: "Why don't you go back to Boise and forget about the while thing? I don't think it is a very advisable subject to discuss. I have discontinued talking about it with anyone."

After some persuasion, he did come up to the hotel. He related the following story:

On June 21, 1947, in the afternoon about 2:00 o'clock, I was patrolling the east bay of Maury Island close

in to the shore. This uninhabited island lies directly opposite the city of Tacoma about three miles from the mainland. This day the sea was rather bumpy and there were numerous low-hanging clouds. I, as captain, was steering my patrol boat close to the shore of a bay on Maury Island. On board were two crewmen, my fifteen-year-old son and his dog.

As I looked up from the wheel on my boat I noticed six very large doughnut-shaped aircraft. I would judge they were at about 2,000 feet above the water and almost directly overhead. At first glance I thought them to be balloons as they seemed to be stationary. However upon further observance, five of these strange aircraft were circling very slowly around the sixth one which was stationary in the center of the formation. It appeared to me that the center aircraft was in some kind of trouble as it was losing altitude fairly rapidly. The other aircraft stayed at a distance of 200 feet above the center one as if they were following the center one down. The center aircraft came to rest almost directly overhead at about 500 feet above the water.

All on board our boat were watching these aircraft with a great deal of interest as they apparently had no motor, propellers, or any visual signs of propulsion, and to the best of our hearing they made no sound. In describing the aircraft, I would say they were at least 100 feet in diameter. Each had a hole in the center, approximately 25 feet in diameter. They were all a sort of shell-like gold and silver color. Their surface seemed of metal and appeared to be burled, because when the light shone on them through the clouds they were brilliant, not all one brilliance, but many brilliances, something like a Buick dashboard. All of the aircraft seemed to have large portholes equally spaced around the outside of their doughnut exterior. These portholes were from five to six feet in diameter and were round. They also appeared to have a dark, circular, continuous window on the inside and bottom of their doughnut shape as though it were an observatior window.

All of us aboard the boat were afraid this center balloon was going to crash in the bay, and just a little while before it stopped lowering, we had pulled out boat over to the beach and got out with our harbor patrol camera. I took three or four photographs of these balloons.

The center balloon-like aircraft remained stationary at about 500 feet from the water while the other five aircraft kept circling over it. After about five or six minutes one of the aircraft from the circling formation left its place in the formation and lowered itself down right next to the stationary aircraft. In fact, it appeared to touch it and stayed stationary next to the center aircraft as if it were giving some kind of assistance for about three or four minutes.

It was then we heard a dull thud, like an underground explosion or a thud similar to a man stamping his heel on damp ground. Immediately following this sound the center aircraft began spewing forth what seemed like thousands of newspapers from somewhere on the inside of its center. These newspapers, which turned out to be a white type of very light-weight metal, fluttered to earth, most of them lighting in the bay. It then seemed to hail on us, in the bay and over the beach, black or darker type metal which looked similar to lava rock. We did not know if this metal was coming from the aircraft, but assumed that it was, as it fell at the same time that the white type metal was still falling. However, since these fragments were of a darker color, we did not observe them until they started hitting the beach and the bay. All of these latter fragments seemed very hot, almost molten. When they hit the bay, steam rose from the water.

We ran for shelter under a cliff on the beach and behind logs to protect ourselves from the falling debris. In spite of our precaution, my son's arm was injured by one of the falling fragments and our dog was hit and killed. We buried the dog at sea on our return trip to Tacoma.

After this rain of metal seemed over, all of these strange aircraft lifted slowly and drifted out to the westward, which is out to sea. They rose and disappeared at a tremendous height. The center aircraft, which had spewed the debris, did not seem to be hindered in its flight and still remained in the center of the formation as they all rose and disappeared out to sea.

We tried to pick up several pieces of the metal or fragments and found them very hot—in fact, I almost burned my fingers—but after some of them had cooled we loaded a considerable number of the pieces aboard the boat. We also picked up some of the metal which had looked like falling newspapers.

My crew and I discussed this observance for awhile and I attempted to radio from my patrol boat back to my base. The static was so great it was impossible for me to reach my radio station. This I attributed to the presence of these aircraft, as my radio had been in perfect operating order and the weather would not have caused this amount of interference.

The wheelhouse on our boat had been hit by the falling debris and damaged. We immediately started our engines and went directly to Tacoma, where my boy was given first aid at the hospital there. Upon reaching dock I had to tell my superior officer how the boat had been damaged and why the dog had not returned with us. I related our experience to Fred L. Crisman, my superior officer. I could plainly see that he did not believe it and I guess I don't blame him, but we gave him the camera with its film and the fragments of metal we had loaded aboard as proof of our story. Fred L. Crisman decided he would at least go out and investigate the beach where I judged at least twenty tons of the debris had fallen.

I might add here that these strange

aircraft appeared completely round, but seemed a little squashed on the top and on the bottom as if you placed a large board on an inner tube and squashed it slightly. The film from our camera, developed, showed these strange aircraft, but the negatives were covered with white spots similar to a negative that has been close to an x-ray room before it has been exposed.

That was the story that was related to me, Kenneth Arnold, by Harold A. Dahl, Captain of the Harbor Patrol of Tacoma, Washington. I give it in Mr. Dahl's words almost verbatim. After Mr. Dahl had related this story, he said he hoped that talking or discussing this matter of his observations was not going to wish any bad luck onto me.

He said that the next morning after he had made his observations, at about seven o'clock a gentleman called at his home and invited him to breakfast. Dahl said that this wasn't particularly unusual because many lumber buyers did call on people in his type of work early in the morning, as many times they wanted to buy salvage logs. This gentleman, Dahl said, wore a dark suit, he looked a lot like an insurance salesman, was about forty years old and was driving a 1947 black Buick sedan. Harold said that he would go to breakfast with him and Harold drove his car, which is a Chrysler, downtown to a little cafe and this other gentleman followed him.

The peculiar thing was that this gentleman did not want to discuss lumber. He was more interested in asking Harold about his family and about personal affairs, and if he was happy in his work and if he would like to continue being pleased and happy with his work and family. Harold thought that was rather unusual and finally asked him what he was getting at and the man, as they were having breakfast, told Harold almost verbatim what he had observed the afternoon before out on Maury Island.

Harold knew, or felt that he knew

in his own mind, that this gentleman couldn't possibly have been out on Maury Island or couldn't possibly have observed these same aircraft, but the man left Harold at breakfast that morning with a sound impression that Harold Dahl ought to forget what he had observed out there and stop talking about it because Harold accidentally had observed something that he shouldn't have observed and that it would be much better for his business, his family and his general welfare not to discuss it with anyone.

Harold said to me: "I didn't put much stock in it but I did think it was rather fantastic how this gentleman happened to know what I had seen and I was quite sure that he hadn't talked to any of my crew and I know he hadn't talked to me before. In fact, I had never seen him before."

The things this gentleman had warned him about sort of revolved in his mind, but when he went back to his dock to continue his business that day of the 22nd of June, he still decided that he would go on discussing it, talking about it, because it was a very unusual experience. Many of the other seamen had asked him questions and he felt as though he should answer them.

Anyhow, Harold said, hard luck started hitting him immediately. A bunch of logs they had salvaged out on the bay turned up missing. He didn't know if they went out with the tide or what happened. He said that it was rather unexplainable. He also said that a few days afterward, his fifteen-year-old son, the one who had been injured in the accident out on Maury Island, had come up missing, and they found him through the sheriff's office in Lusk, Montana. On questioning, his son admitted he did not know why he was there or how he had gotten there and very willingly came back home. Harold said to me that his wife was rather nervous and upset and that her health wasn't of the best which, he said, is not particularly unusual, but it was just that his whole business and home and family all seemed to be going wrong. The

Board of Directors of a lumber company that he had an interest in voted against him on several issues Harold felt confident were going to be a profit to their business, and that had lost him considerable amount of money.

Other incidents he mentioned were inability to get their patrol boats started and they had to be worked on until about noon before they ever got them going, their boats started springing leaks and it seemed like hard luck was just following him around. After this had gone on for a week, he decided that maybe there was something to what the stranger had warned him about. It was because of these happenings he had refused to discuss the matter with anyone and that he was only discussing it with me because I had been more or less the object of criticism because of my observations that did break out through the newspapers.

He said he would be glad to show me several of these fragments he had picked up on Maury Island that had fallen from the strange aircraft. "We've been using them up there for ashtrays." I went with him and he looked around awhile and finally found the fragments and when I first saw them I said:

"Why, Harold, that's only lava rock."

"Well, I don't know much about metals," he said, 'but that's the stuff that came out of the airplane. I know it did. Some of the white metal is over here in a garage of Crisman's. We'll go over and see it if you'd like."

I said: "Oh, that isn't special, I'll see it tomorrow." That evening we talked about this and that, fishing and hunting and about his experiences and all the while he kept reminding me:

"Now that you've heard my story, go on back to Boise and forget about it, so you won't have a run of bad luck like I've had." This bad luck that he was stressing so, he didn't quite associate with his observation, yet he did associate it. He looked like a man who was rather frightened and puzzled about the whole situation.

The next morning about nine-thirty Crisman and Dahl knocked on my hotel room door. I asked Crisman to tell me his story and Fred L. Crisman told me the experience he had had the 23rd of June when he went out to investigate the truthfulness of Harold Dahl's story.

He had taken a harbor patrol boat the 23rd of June, in the morning, out to the island and had observed about twenty tons of debris out there and as he was looking at some of it, one of the strange aircraft came out of somewhere, he wasn't just sure, but it made a circle of the bay and it banked in its circle at about a ten degree angle, circled the bay and went right into the center of a high cumulus cloud or thunder cloud. Crisman said that he had seen a lot of aircraft, but he had never seen them go into the center of a cloud before. It's pretty rough in there!

Crisman continued: "I observed this strange aircraft to be something similar to a balloon. It looked like a large inner tube to me. It didn't look squashed as Harold Dahl had told it, it looked more round, that is doughnut round or inner tube round, and it had large portholes about five feet in diameter that encircled the whole aircraft. It also had the observation window and definitely had a birling effect on its surface. It looked like a metal, a sort of brassy color or golden color, and maybe a little silver mixed in with it; and when the sun shone on it, it did show much more brilliance than would be expected from a polished surface."

Crisman said he tarried there awhile and picked up quite a load of fragments, put them on his boat, and then he returned to his dock in Tacoma. He did confirm the story of Harold Dahl and said that it certainly was true that he had seen one of these strange aircraft which Harold Dahl had seen.

I ordered breakfast up to the room and we sat around discussing this thing pro and con. Crisman seemed rather anxious to show me the pictures that they had taken as well as other fragments, and because he was quite anxious to show me this and to take me out to the island, I began to believe their story and asked both Crisman and Dahl if they would mind if I called army intelligence.

I said: "I think this thing is very serious and I think that it is an investigation that should be conducted by people who are accustomed to investigating things, not by a novice like myself or like yourselves." Crisman agreed with me, and Dahl said, that he didn't care about talking to military intelligence, but "if Crisman wants to, it's okay with me." I also asked them if they would mind if I asked Captain E. J. Smith of United Airlines to come over and listen to the stories. I told them that he more or less was an object of criticism the same as myself and without a doubt this might be tangible evidence that would prove our observations correct and stop a lot of these newspaper stories that had made us the laughing stock of the country. We felt that our integrity was at stake. It wasn't so much the newspaper talk, but when anyone says you're seeing spots or calls you a liar, you get upset about it, especially when you are not used to telling lies or making up some wild tale.

I called military intelligence first and I asked for Lt. Frank M. Brown. Brown, when he found out that it was me calling him, wouldn't take the telephone call collect on the military line. He went to a pay telephone to call me. Why, I don't really know. Anyhow, I told Frank Brown that I had something interesting to relate to him up here and that I had some fragments of what I thought was a flying disk and said: "If you fellows could come up, I think your trip probably would be worthwhile. I have enough evidence, in my own mind, to give real credence to what I ran into up here in Tacoma." I didn't describe these aircraft to Frank M. Brown to any degree at all, that is, I didn't describe any details about them that Harold Dahl and Fred Crisman had

seen, but in spite of that Frank M. Brown was very interested.

He said: "If we don't call you back within an hour, we'll be there."

After I finished that phone call, I called Captain E. J. Smith. The first time I called Captain Smith, he wasn't in, but finally I did reach him about twelve-thirty or one o'clock and I did tell Captain Smith over the phone a more or less brief of the story that had been related to me by Crisman and Dahl and about the fragments. Smith seemed intensely interested. I told him that I would fly over to Seattle and pick him up that afternoon if he would care to come over and listen to these stories. Fred Crisman took me down to the airport about three-thirty. I took off for Seattle to pick up Captain Smith at about four o'clock. Captain Smith was there and we had a cup of coffee and I related a little further the information that I had received from these two men over at Tacoma. Captain Smith became more and more interested and wanted to come over immediately, so we both got in my ship and I took off for Tacoma. At the hotel, I went directly up to the room and Crisman and Smith went out somewhere. I was in the hotel room alone about five-thirty or six o'clock that day of Thursday, July 31, 1947, when Frank M. Brown called me from the desk and said that he and Captain Davidson had flown up to Tacoma in a B-25 Bomber and wanted to talk to me. I immediately invited them up to the room.

When they got up to my room, which was 502, I more or less jumped all over them in this respect. I said: "You fellows like to know a lot of things but you won't tell me anything. I'm awfully curious about this thing because this has happened to me and it hasn't happened to you yet. I hope you can appreciate how I feel. I've got something here very interesting that I want to tell you about and to show you and I want you to talk to these men because I think their story has some base to it, but before I do this, I would like to have you fellows, just as man to man, tell e what you have found out since you profess you have never seen a flying disk, and you don't know anything about them, but that you feel that they probably do exist and you are interested in information. You've done nothing but investigate this thing since the 24th of June; how about giving me a little of that information? At least for my own personal satisfaction."

Captain Davidson asked me to come over and sit on the bed where he took a pencil and piece of paper and drew me some pictures. He said: "We have several photographs in our Intelligence Department that were taken by a man in his front yard in Phoenix, Arizona, that are authentic. They are pictures and good pictures of these flying saucers or flying disks. I am drawing you here, Mr. Arnold, the photographs that we have in our possession."

He drew me a picture. First, of an almost round object that had a dark circle in the center of it and made this remark: "It apparently seems, according to the negative, that this flying disk had a hole in the center of it, or it could be a hole in the center of it."

I was being very much convinced by this time.

Then he drew another picture. This picture was really quite a shock to me. He drew a picture of a half-moon that had a sort of a half peak in the center of it. It was all rounded, easy flowing lines, and this picture was of another type of disk. This is the peculiar part of it and the reason I was shocked. On June 24th when I made my observation of the nine flying disks, the second one from the bottom looked just exactly like the picture he drew. The reason that I had never mentioned it or even talked about it or said anything to anyone about this peculiar shaped disk was that I thought the angle that I was looking from was the reason why the second one from the bottom in this formation looked like the one they drew in their picture, but upon reviewing my observation carefully, I feel that if that one had looked like that picture, all of them would have looked the same which, of course, they didn't. They had a convex angle at the tail instead of a more or less concave angle rounded in shape. The peculiar object which they drew is four times as wide as it is long and the tips of its wings are rather bat-like and its center or fuselage is exactly the same length as the tips of the wings.

I knew right then and there that whether Davidson and Brown had ever seen any of these flying disks, they were getting pretty close to finding out all the information that could be found out about them, as none of them had actually fallen any place to my knowledge. After they had finished drawing me those pictures, we waited for another half hour or so discussing various features of this mysterious thing until Crisman and Smith came in. Dahl didn't take part in the conversation with military intelligence. He had work to do at home, or something, and he wasn't too anxious to talk to them anyhow. Why, I don't know. Crisman related his complete story to Captain Davidson. Captain Davidson and Lieutenant Brown saw the pile of fragments that were on the floor and handled some of them. Our discussion lasted until about twelve-thirty when both Brown and Davidson decided that they had to get back to Hamilton Field because they were short of airplanes and that they had to have every airplane in the air for a big air show that was going to come off the next day, and even though Captain Smith and myself tried to persuade them to stay over and see the island for additional proof of the truth of Dahl's and Crisman's story, they insisted on leaving that night. Crisman gave them, and both Smith and I helped them load a whole Kellogg's corn flake box full of flying disk fragments from Maury Island into the rear trunk of the army taxi car that came to get them from McChord Field. They seemed to have cooled off on our story. Smith and I thought there was so much evidence that indicated the story was true that we couldn't quite understand their attitude for not wanting to see the island or for not wanting to stay there longer and do more investigating. They did want the samples, but their excuse for getting back to Hamilton Field seemed rather a feeble excuse considering the fact that their job of investigating flying disks was quite important. We knew it was important because we know that they exist.

Captain Smith stayed with me that night of July 31, Thursday. Smith and I discussed many phases of this while we were in bed and there seemed to be a lot of evidence to prove that Crisman's and Dahl's story was absolutely true and yet there was a lot of evidence that didn't quite add up and we couldn't piece it together. We knew something very strange was going on. All during the conference we had been bothered by the United Press and Paul Lance of *Tacoma Times* telling us what some mysterious telephone informant was telling them. It seemed that there was a certain person who kept calling the United Press telling them what was going on in Room 502 at the Winthrop Hotel, and the fantastic thing was that everything he said to the press that was going on up in room 502 at the Winthrop Hotel was true.

I don't know about later predictions that he made but I will relate to you that the press someway, somehow, found out that I was in town. They also found out that Captain Smith was there. They found out that we were investigating some flying disk fragments that were obtained through Fred L. Crisman and Harold A. Dahl of the Tacoma Harbor Patrol. Ted Morello, the United Press correspondent, told us very plainly over the phone, and several times after we had met him, that we were engaged in a very serious affair. His informants couldn't get the information that they generally can get on any kind of a story and Morello told us: "When my informants can't get

me this information that I need and want, brother, there is something very serious going on, and I would suggest that Smith and Arnold, both of you, better get out of this town or go someplace and don't become involved."

That was rather peculiar because some of that conversation happened before the B-25 bomber crashed. Anyhow, we didn't want to talk to the press. Why should we? If Crisman's and Dahl's story was proven to be some kind of a hoax, Smith and I would both be the laughing stock of the country, and if it didn't prove to be any kind of a hoax, we had everything to win and nothing to lose. We weren't having a very good time because of this mysterious telephone informant, the press finding out almost verbatim what our conversations were, and so on. We looked in our room for tapped wires, and couldn't find anything that showed that any information was creeping out.

At one time, Ted Morello, United Press correspondent, called us and said: "We have this mysterious telephone informant on the other line here at the Tacoma *Times*." Both Crisman and Dahl were in the room with Smith and myself. The mysterious telephone informant was telling Ted Morello what we were talking about in that room. The room wasn't tapped in any way that we knew of it and we did really search— tore the pictures off the wall, tore up the rugs, tore the beds apart. We were beginning to get worried. The situation was getting rather "spooky."

Smith and I went to sleep that night of July 31st. We woke up in the morning about nine o'clock when we heard the telephone ring. It was Fred Crisman. He said: "Have you heard the news this morning? A B-25 bomber crashed this morning at about 2:30 a.m. I have checked McChord Field and there was only one B-25 that left. You know and I know who was aboard that airplane!"

We heard through Crisman that morning that both the pilot and the co-pilot were killed, but that two other men, a chief engineer and a passenger, had parachuted to safety. Smith verified all this information at McChord Field. We found that the bomber had been under military guard while Lieutenant Frank M. Brown and Captain Davidson were interviewing us at the Hotel Winthrop. We also found out that the two men who parachuted from the plane were ordered to parachute by the co-pilot who strapped chutes on them and forced them out the door. The plane did not crash until eleven minutes later. This was found out through the United Press and their informants.

Ted Morello let us listen to the first recording of one of the men who had parachuted to safety and who was slightly injured. It was the passenger. This boy told the story that the left engine of the B-25 burst into flame all at once and that it happened about twenty minutes after the take-off. It was also mentioned that the chief engineer had said that the automatic fire fighting apparatus installed in this airplane had failed to function.

There was a sheriff at Kelso who watched the plane in the air and saw it crash. The description this man gave the press was that the plane was observed at quite a high altitude with the left engine on fire. Its wings, tail and fuselage were intact. It turned, went into a very steep dive and crashed into the hillside. This steep dive lasted for quite some time before the crash.

If a man is conscious and his airplane is on fire, the first thought any pilot would have is to try to slow that airplane up, as slow as possible, because he would rather crash at 90 miles an hour than 250 or 300 miles an hour. Their plane was intact; tail, rudder surfaces and wings. I know both of these pilots and I saw their licenses. They were pilots of the highest type of ability and would have slowed up that airplane before they crashed. Were both of these men dead long before their plane actually crashed and that is the reason their plane was under little or no control?

Further, this airplane was equipped with the finest type of radio devices. They did not radio or attempt to radio anyone that their engine was on fire or that the plane was in trouble. Twelve hours before Army Intelligence released the names of the two intelligence officers killed in this crash, the mysterious telephone informant did tell the press their names, where they had come, what they were doing, their destination and what they were carrying aboard their B-25. Everything that this mysterious telephone informant said to the press was true to the very best of my knowledge. I am confident that no one of the four of us that were left in this investigation that next day of August 1st, had talked to the press or had even told the press the names of people or parties who were visiting us or what we were discussing. Friday morning at ten o'clock, we made an arrangement with Fred Crisman to board his patrol boat and go out to Maury Island to see the fragments that we were told about; they told us there was about twenty tons more of it out there on the island. Smith and I discussed it to some extent before we went down to the boat, but we decided we would still investigate or try to get at the bottom of this if we could. We went down to the boat with Fred Crisman. We attempted to start the motor in the boat and the motor would not start. Crisman's mechanic was working on the motor. They had no other patrol boat available so Crisman suggested that in about an hour the mechanic would probably have the boat going and we'd all come back down to the boat and take off for Maury Island. We looked over the supposed damage to the boat. We could see that the boat had been damaged some. We didn't know to what extent, but it wasn't quite as great an extent as we felt that Crisman had impressed us that it had been damaged. We could see that the window had been replaced and a horn and other things about the boat had been replaced. Smith and I went back to the hotel and waited for Crisman to call us at about eleven o'clock. He didn't call and we waited until two-thirty or three o'clock that afternoon, then finally called Harold Dahl and asked why Crisman hadn't called us and asked if he would look up Crisman and find out what had happened to him. Then Ted Morello of the United Press called us and told us that one of the four men in the room that morning, which would have been Dahl, Crisman, Smith or I, was going to be on an Army bomber headed for Alaska that afternoon. When we heard that tip from Ted Morello we immediately got hot on trying to find Crisman. We did locate Dahl finally and he did locate a note that was left by Fred Crisman that said he was going to be gone for two or three days on a business trip. It seemed very peculiar that Crisman didn't call us and tell us that or it may be that he couldn't. We don't know. We were expecting most anything to happen. United Press called us again and said that this mysterious telephone informant was now predicting things: "Captain Smith would be called Tuesday, August 5, to Wright Field, Dayton, Ohio, to be interrogated by the Military Intelligence." . . . "Kenneth Arnold's plane had been shot at in the air flying over the states of Washington and Oregon on numerous occasions." . . . "Captain Smith's airline had also been shot at on numerous occasions over one of the western states." Also: "The B-25 bomber was shot down by a 20mm cannon."

The mysterious telephone informant also said that "The C-40 Marine plane that had crashed into the southwest side of Mt. Ranier (that was the plane I was searching for the day that I first made my observation of the flying disks), when discovered and actually investigated, would reveal that this ship had also been shot down and it had been shot down because there were certain people aboard this ship who had information in their possession that "they" didn't want to get out to anyone."

(Editor's note: This Marine C-46

was found on July 26 on the 10,000-foot level of South Tacoma Glacier, near Longmire, Washington. Eight men who climbed the glacier, discovered the wreckage. "Everywhere we looked there were parts of the plane," Ranger George Senner reported. But the searching party found none of the bodies of the 32 marines who were aboard when the transport crashed. $5,000 reward offered by relatives of the dead men was never paid, apparently, because of this unaccountable fact. No evidence of sabotage or "shooting down" could be discovered.)

Ted Morello told me that this mysterious informant had also told him that the United Airlines ship that crashed on LaGuardia Field (now solved by authorities who discovered that the controls had been locked), was sabotaged and that the plane that had crashed in Copenhagen some many months ago on takeoff, also had been sabotaged.

We got it now—or thought we did. We were being given the "works" by some person. We were being made to look ridiculous. Further, we were getting nowhere with our investigation. We had not gotten out to Maury Island; we never seemed able to get the pictures taken by Dahl of the flying disks—Crisman mentioned they were in his mountain cabin 55 miles up in the hills. We decided we had better go home. But we made one more try.

We met Harold and his secretary, stopped for breakfast at a little roadside tavern. While we were at breakfast Captain Smith went to the telephone and called somebody. I didn't know at the time who he called. This was Sunday morning, August 3rd. He came back to the table and said that he had an appointment with someone and that I should wait for him at the hotel and he would be back at twelve o'clock. I went back to the hotel room and waited until almost one-thirty before Captain Smith showed up, and when he did show up he was with Major Sanders of McChord Field, S-2 Intelligence. Captain Smith asked me to relate my story to Major Sanders. I did this as briefly as possible.

Captain Smith said: "The reason I asked you to tell Major Sanders this is because I wanted him to hear our stories separately, and I wanted to find out just exactly what the score was—whether we should leave or whether A-2 wanted to interroga e us."

When I had finished giving this description to Major Sanders he got up and looked at the fragments and said: "That's nothing but smelter slag. I'll tell you what it is. It's just some kind of a hoax. That's true."

He said: "Now, I know that these flying disks exist although I've never seen one. I don't know what the objects of Crisman and Dahl are, but these fragments they have given you are nothing but slag from the local smelter.

Smith took a piece of the fragments home with him to use as a paper weight on his desk. I was going to take one of the fragments and use it as an ashtray just to remind me of the experience I had in Tacoma. But Major Sanders very carefully took every piece and asked to have the pieces we had picked up, too. He wrapped them all in a towel and put it in his car. Then Sanders decided to take us out to the smelter and show us thousands of tons of material very similar to this or just exactly like it. He did take us out and we did see some black fragments and smelter slag that did look a lot like the substance that we had. It was heavy and I think to some degree Captain Smith was convinced that the fragments we had were or could very easily be smelter slag.

The foregoing information, supplied us by Mr. Kenneth Arnold, is supplemented with photostats of the following letters, which were sent to him by *The Seattle Times:*

The Seattle Times
Seattle 41, Washington
Sept. 4, 1947

Mr. Kenneth Arnold,
Boise, Idaho

Dear Mr. Arnold:

Attached is a volunteered copy of a letter from the commanding general of the Fourth Air Force. I believe it will still some of the apprehension you voiced in our long-distance telephone conversation a week or so ago.

I hadn't asked General Hale for copies of his reassuring letter, but the fact that he provided me with several seems to indicate complete cooperation on the part of the Army, and their willingness for you to say whatever you like.

In the event of your coming to Seattle soon, I'd appreciate a talk with you—off the record, if you insist. If you don't plan to be over, couldn't you drop me a note, also confidentially if you prefer, just sketching your correspondence with whatever publication it was in Illinois which asked for a flying disk story? I'd appreciate knowing the name of the magazine, in any case, and the name of the man with whom you corresponded.

And would you please include the street address of your home or business office?

Very truly yours,
Robert Heilman,
City news staff

Office of the Commanding General
Headquarters Fourth Air Force
Hamilton Field, California
August 25, 1947

Mr. Henry MacLeod,
The Seattle Times,
Seattle, Washington
Dear Mr. MacLeod:

Your letter of August 21, 1947, to Lt. Col. Donald Springer of this headquarters, has been brought to my attention.

You are advised that I have no knowledge of the origination of the flying disk stories. My Intelligence personnel have had several pertinent incidents brought to their attention by civilian and government agencies. For your information, this headquarters, in the interest of economy, does not intend to pursue each and every reported flying disk. However, in the interest of national defense, reliable reports of such a nature will be investigated.

I have no knowledge at this time of any statement to be made by a government agency regarding the flying disk.

As you know, there is no censorship on individuals within the United States, therefore, you may feel free to interrogate Mr. Arnold, Capt. Smith, or whomever you desire. I have no authentic information which would indicate that those individuals, or any other persons, should maintain secrecy regarding their alleged observations.

Sincerely yours,
Willis H. Hale.
Major General, U. S. Army,
Commanding

From the evidence presented in this article, the editors conclude that the flying disks cannot be a hoax, because if they are, it is a hoax which involves a tremendous operation, perfect coordination and an enormous financial expenditure. In other words, it is imposible to call this a hoax.

An alternative, of course, is that these things *are* a military development; but if they are, it is one which our military services disdain to keep secret. It would seem apparent that military observers *are* much interested in the disks, however. Their interest may be on the basis of foreign powers being behind the disks. But the scope of the observations, hundreds of them perfectly reliable, rule this out also. The mere scientific know-how involved is far beyond our own technological advance, perhaps for hundreds of years to come.

What, then, are the flying disks?

Are the pulp magazines, purveyors of ray guns and rocket ships from Mars, proving prophetic? Are these mysterious craft ships from other planets in our solar system? Is H. G. Wells' "War of The Worlds" a reality at last? Are we facing an invasion from space?

The answer your editors have arrived at is NO.

These disks, no matter how logical it may seem that they may conceivably have been instrumental in causing certain aircraft crashes in this and other countries, have been proven to be void of ill-intent. They have appeared for hundreds of years all over the world. The flying disk story which for two weeks swept the newspapers into a frenzy of misstatement, contradiction and pure imagination is not a new one. It has happened before! Especially during the past forty years, reports have come in steadily from all over the world, of large disk-shaped aircraft, of wheel-like submersibles in very deep ocean water, of mysterious round or semi-round objects in space, observed by reputable astronomers and duly reported in astronomical journals.

If, then, these objects have been with us so long, we have little to fear from them now. And if they are peopled by intelligent beings, as seems so obvious from the extreme scientific principles which must lie behind their construction and navigation, it may not be hard to understand their unwillingness to contact a race of people who engage constantly in the horrible slaughter we call war, and who live in the crime-filled centers we call cities.

However, this is all conjecture. The real facts are these: The flying disks exist. They are a matter of vital concern to us, friendly or otherwise. They are appearing in enormous numbers, far beyond any appearances heretofore recorded. They must be here for a definite reason. Their actions are integrated. Their pattern of appearances show specific intent. There is concrete evidence in the form of fragments which are definitely not slag from a smelter (at least not *all* of them). There is also an irritating element of sabotage and subterfuge involved in research both private and military concerning the flying disks. Two men are known to have died investigating a matter which they considered of top importance, above and beyond all their other work. And lastly, almost daily appearances of one type of flying object or other are being reported, and are the objects of a self-imposed censorship by most newspapers through fear of further ridicule; and worst of all, reliable observations are being lost through the same fear.

We therefore urge, without a personal axe to grind, that all persons who can give competent evidence of flying disks, do so immediately, contacting military authorities, or this magazine, as you desire. It may be important. And military authorities, have a file—they will not be averse to adding to it. Certainly it can do no harm.

Allow us, in our turn (Kenneth Arnold, Captain E. J. Smith, and thousands of others) to indulge in a huge belly-laugh at the expense of those noted "authorities" who so smugly ridiculed us for "spots before our eyes."

At least we've seen the spots!

www.ingramcontent.com/pod-product-compliance
Lightning Source LLC
Chambersburg PA
CBHW080734020726
47503CB00010B/2909